# Rise to Power 2

T.J. Edwards

**Lock Down Publications and Ca$h Presents**
# Rise to Power 2
**A Novel by *T.J. Edwards***

Rise to Power 2

# Lock Down Publications
P.O. Box 870494
Mesquite, Tx 75187

Copyright 2019 Rise to Power 2

**Lock Down Publications**
**Like our page on Facebook: Lock Down Publications @**
www.facebook.com/lockdownpublications.ldp
Cover design and layout by: **Dynasty Cover Me**
Book interior design by: **Shawn Walker**
Edited by: **Kiera Northington**

T.J. Edwards

# Stay Connected with Us!

Text **LOCKDOWN** to 22828 to stay up-to-date with new releases, sneak peaks, contests and more…
Or CLICK HERE to sign up.

Thank you!

# Like our page on Facebook:

**Lock Down Publications:** Facebook

**Join** Lock Down Publications/The New Era Reading Group

# Follow us on Instagram:

**Lock Down Publications:** Instagram

Email Us: We want to hear from you!

## Submission Guideline.

Submit the first three chapters of your completed manuscript to ldpsubmissions@gmail.com, subject line: Your book's title. The manuscript must be in a .doc file and sent as an attachment. Document should be in Times New Roman, double spaced and in size 12 font. Also, provide your synopsis and full contact information. If sending multiple submissions, they must each be in a separate email.

Have a story but no way to send it electronically? You can still submit to LDP/Ca$h Presents. Send in the first three chapters, written or typed, of your completed manuscript to:

LDP: Submissions Dept
Po Box 870494
Mesquite, Tx 75187

*DO NOT send original manuscript. Must be a duplicate.*

Provide your synopsis and a cover letter containing your full contact information.

Thanks for considering LDP and Ca$h Presents.

T.J. Edwards

# Rise to Power 2

## Chapter 1

### Kaleb

I tipped toe to the door and peered out the peephole. The sight of Gorilla's double barrel shotgun pressed under Buddy's chin, made the hairs on my arms stand on end. He had it pressed so tight that even through the peephole, I could see a trickle of blood forming around the portion of the steel connected to Buddy's skin.

"Yo, son, if I have to tell you to open this door again, I'm about to blow ya man's shits all over this hallway, then we gon' kick in that door and fuck you over too. That's my word. All I'm asking for is a sit-down. Don't turn this shit into a murder scene," Gorilla growled.

He was every bit of six feet, five inches tall. Dark-skinned and real muscular, with a gut. He had four men that stood behind him, armed with red rags covering half of their faces. They were supposed to be my Blood niggas, but me and Buddy hadn't been fucking wit them in almost a year. After killing one of the heads that ran the mob, we'd gone AWOL and started to do our own things.

"Yo, take that gun away from my nigga, Gorilla. Do that and me and you can rap for a minute. You ain't gotta have my mans hemmed up like that," I said, looking through the peephole.

Bree stepped from the back room, wearing a pair of tight jogging pants that conformed to her thick thighs. She had on a pink beater that showcased her braless breasts. The cones of her areolas were visible through the fabric. The jogging pants were all up in her gap. Her camel toe was present. She was barefoot, her toes were French-tipped and freshly pedicured. She looked real good, even considering the circumstances. No more than an hour prior, I'd just climbed from between her thighs, hitting that pussy from as many angles as my stamina allowed.

As I looked down the hallway at her, I was feeling guilty again, because Buddy was my right-hand man and best friend. And Bree was his baby mother. A female he was crazy about. We been fucking around behind his back and things were starting to take an emotional turn. I waved her back into the room.

"Kaleb, who's at the door?" she asked in a loud whisper. She looked scared. Her pretty brown eyes were opened wide. Her bottom lip trembled before she placed her index finger inside it, biting nervously.

I waved her off once again and turned back to the peephole. Gorilla dragged Buddy in front of the door and cocked the double barrel. "Son, you got thirty seconds to open this door or ya man gets it. Count down." He mugged the peephole and looked down at Buddy. "Some type of friend that nigga is, Buddy. Kid won't even open the door to ya life. Fifteen seconds, lil nigga."

I placed my back on the door and closed my eyes. Took a deep breath and tried to think things over logically. There were five of them in all. Four hittas, plus Gorilla. But, Gorilla's gun was jammed up against Buddy's chin. The other dudes all looked to have handguns of seventeen shots or less. I had a nine millimeter with thirteen shots, and a clip of an additional thirteen in my back pocket. I had Bree in the back room, defenseless. She was not only my right-hand man's baby mother, but she was the mother to my goddaughter, Breeyonna, a little four-year-old girl that had my heart already. On top of that, I would never forgive myself if I allowed anything to happen to Bree.

I had thoughts of opening the door and just bussing until my clip was empty, gunning them niggas down, but I ran the risk of losing Buddy in the process, and getting hit up myself. I didn't know what to do. But, I couldn't leave my nigga out there to fend for his self. I was already responsible for having his left hand get cut off. Not to mention, I was fucking and doing a lot of nasty shit with his baby mother behind his back. Man, I was in a dilemma.

I could hear Gorilla counting down loudly. I wondered if any of the occupants in the building had already called the police. But then again, this was New York, where everybody minded their own business and stayed in their own lanes. I waited until I heard him get to eight, before I placed my hand on the lock, and took a deep breath. *Fuck it, here goes nothing*, I thought, clutching the handle of my gun tightly. "Aiight, Gorilla. I'm about to open this bitch. Just chill out, nigga." I undid the chain, then moved my hand downward to the next lock, when I heard tires come screeching to a halt outside.

I rushed over to the window and saw four black trucks pull up, before a bunch of niggas with long nappy dreads, and their native flag covering half of their faces jumped out. They reached into their trucks and came up with titanium-colored assault rifles. Cocked them back and rushed up to the building, looking both ways. My eyes got as big as paper plates. I backed away from the window and almost tripped, trying to turn around. Stumbled and banged my knee into Bree's living room table. It started to bleed right away. "Fuck! Bree! Bree! Throw yo shoes on, ma!" I hollered, rushing toward the back room, just as the shots from outside started to rain rapidly, shattering her windows and putting big holes in the walls. Plaster poofed into the air in white clouds of smoke, choking me. I dropped down to my knees, then shot up and ran into her bedroom, bussing through the door with my right shoulder.

She screamed at the top of her lungs. Covered her head with her arms. She tucked in between her dresser and queen sized bed. She had on one pink and black AirMax 90s, on her way to put the other one on. "What's going on? Is that Buddy shooting at my house?" she screamed.

*Boom. Boom. Boom. Pop. Pop. Pop.*

*Doom. Doom. Doom. Boom. Boom.*

More rapid fire.

More windows shattering.

I fell to the ground and low-crawled over to her, hugged her to my body until there was a break in the gun shower. She was shaking like crazy.

"Bree, calm down. I got you, ma. I got you. We about to get the fuck up out of here. You hear me? All

I'm asking is that you don't freak out."

As soon as I said this, there was so much rapid fire that I could hear pictures falling off of her wall, to the floor. The glass tables in her house were broken and by this time, all of the windows were hit. The apartment filled with smoke and debris. I didn't know if the dread heads from Jamaica were solely bussing at us, or if Gorilla and his Blood niggas had joined in on the attack. If that was so, I was sure Gorilla had murdered Buddy. Murdered my right-hand man and best friend.

Before I was able to confirm that, I felt myself developing a heavy heart for my homie. There was a brief pause in the shots, then I heard somethin' drop into the front of the house. It sounded like a heavy brick. The heavy scent of gun powder wafted into the air. It was so heavy, I couldn't breathe. Bree coughed harshly and spit on the carpet.

"Come on, Kaleb. Let's get the fuck out of here," she said in a strained voice. She stood up and tried to help me to my feet.

*Bloom*!

The front room exploded and the impact sent us both flying into the wall in her bedroom. I crashed into it so hard, I heard my shoulder crunch. Then, the house was on fire. Big flames consumed the front portion of the hallway, slowly making their way back to where we were. There was a strong stench of burnt copper, and so much smoke that my eyes were burning.

Bree crawled on her knees, with tears running down her cheeks. She coughed and hacked up a spit bubble. Her nose ran. "They are trying to kill us, Kaleb. They're trying to kill us." She sounded as if she were on the verge of breaking into a coughing fit again.

More rapid shots were fired into the apartment. The flames got bigger and bigger. It felt like we were being pushed into an oven. I was sweating profusely. My head and shoulder were throbbing. I waited until the shots paused again. Looked to my right and saw Bree had fallen to her knees, coughing badly. I knelt down, pulled her arm around my neck, and helped her up. Wrapped my left arms around her waist.

"Come on, shorty, we gon' hit it out the back door. Luckily, I'm parked behind your brownstone. Come on," I said through a strained voice. My chest was on fire. The flames were now as tall as me and getting closer. It was so hot in her apartment, my skin felt like somebody was holding a blow dryer to it.

Bree allowed her body to rest against mine. I held her and we rushed into the hallway and ran through the flames there. The walls were on fire and so badly damaged, I could make out the wood behind them. Big holes were in the walls. Everywhere I looked, there were pictures on fire on the floor. As we made our way out of the hallway, Bree reached down to the floor and grabbed a picture of Breeyonna when she was first born. In the picture, she held an Elmo doll in her new arms. Her eyes were opened wide with a big toothless grin on her face.

To the kitchen and straight to the back door, we ran. The entertainment system fell over and crashed to the floor with a loud bang. Bree looked back and started to get sick. "They've destroyed everything I own. What am I going to do? How do I bounce back from this?" she whimpered.

I opened the locks to the back door and pulled the door open. We rushed down the stairs, just as the flames entered the kitchen, looking to cook us to death. My clothes were sticking to me, full of sweat because of the heat. We made it to the stairs and rushed down them, headed toward the exit.

More shots fired.

Because of the fire, the neighbors in the building were rushing out of their apartments and fleeing toward safety. Some of them tumbled down the stairs in their haste to get out of the burning building. Bree stayed close to me, hugged to my chest, while I held her tight and led the way. Police sirens appeared in the far distance. There were the sounds of tires skirting away from the curb, and panicked screams from the other occupants of the building.

When we made it outside, Bree took in a gasp of fresh air and held her chest, coughing until her face was red. Her eyes bugged out of her head. She fell to the grass on her knees, struggling to breathe. I watched the neighbors file out of the building, coughing and choking just as bad as she was. My chest was burning as well. My throat tight, but I knew we had to get out of there quick. The dread heads were looney. They had just proven that. And, they were working with some serious weaponry. They were not only trying to kill us, but they were trying to bake us to death. They meant business and if I was going to enter into a war with them on some deadly shit, then I had to get just as crazy. I was still wondering if my nigga, Buddy, had made it out of the fog.

I helped Bree into my passenger's seat and slammed the door. Rushed around to my driver's side, started the engine and slammed on the gas, just as the police appeared at the front of the building, along with the fire department.

"I'm about to get you out of here, Bree. You coming wit me." I stopped at the end of the alley and made a hard left, stepping on the gas again.

She looked down at the picture of Breeyonna. "What have y'all gotten yourselves into, Kaleb? Don't tell me Gorilla did all of that." She looked over at me with tears in her eyes, before she wiped them away.

"Yo, fuck that nigga Gorilla, man. Son ain't holding like that. That was them fucking Jamaicans. Somebody gave them some bad intel, now they're coming at me and Buddy because of it," I snapped, flying on to the expressway. My chest heaved up and down. My vision was getting a bit hazy, because I was heated and ready to kill up some shit.

Them punk-ass Jamaicans could have easily killed both of us, and all because they thought me and Buddy had killed a boat full of their women that were transporting heroin in their bellies. In actuality, the nigga Sheek, who was originally head of the mission, had done it. He and two of his men. He'd expected me and Buddy assist him, but we didn't. Before Buddy could ice any one of the broads, I'd hit Sheek's ass up. Murdered him, while Buddy hit his men. I wasn't with killing defenseless women, but I didn't have no problem taking half of a nigga's head off, like I was splitting his shit with somebody.

Bree shook her head from left to right. "Damn, I don't want to be a part of this, Kaleb. I got a little girl to think about. Them niggas came to my house with all that shit. Fuck. That means I'm smack dead in the middle." She lowered her head and blew air out of her jaws.

I sat my nine millimeter on my lap. "I ain't about to let nothing happen to you. I got you, Bree. For now, I'm about to put you up with me and Rayven for a few weeks, until we can figure this shit out. I need to make sure you're safe at all times."

"What about Breeyonna? I gotta believe she is a target now too. They probably trying to hit up everybody they even think is involved with the two of you."

"Yo, Breeyonna is under my domain too. I ain't about to let nothin happen to her either. You got my word on that." I squeezed her thigh and tried my best to give her a look that let her know I was serious. I cared about both of them and the man in me wouldn't allow anything to happen to either one if I could prevent it.

"Thank you, Kaleb. One of these days, I'll be able to repay you. It's just that right now I don't have anything. I mean, I just lost everything I had, literally." She lowered her head, and hugged the picture to her chest. The frame was cracked and I was surprised it hadn't broken all the way.

"Yeah, well, don't even worry about all that material stuff. At least you made it out with your life. Besides, I got you. Everything you had in that crib, I'm about to upgrade for you, and then some. I know your swag, ma. I won't let you down. You got me. You understand that?" I glanced over at her, before placing my eyes back on the road. I could see a bunch of traffic looming ahead, so I got off at the next exit and took an alternative route. I needed to get to my crib, so I could collect my thoughts. I was glad that not even Buddy knew where I laid my head. Real bosses never allowed even their closest of close friends to know where they laid their head. I was on my way to becoming a major boss, so I was implementing boss strategies already.

Bree took a deep breath and looked over to me. "Kaleb, what are we going to do about Rayven? All that girl gon' have to do is look into my eyes and she gon' know I'm crazy about you. I can't hide that shit no more. You got this crazy effect on me and I feel like I possess you. I know that don't sound right, but it's the truth. I know y'all are en-gaged and all that, but in my eyes, you belong to me." She grabbed my hand and kissed the back of it.

"Don't worry about Rayven, she and I are going to have to get an understanding about everything. I just gotta find the right time. For now, we're going to get you situated. Clean, safe, and we'll get Breeyonna over to you. I want you to take my laptop and start to look for a crib. When you find one you like, I'll take care of the rent for a year. I got you." I stepped on the gas.

T.J. Edwards

## Chapter 2

It had been three weeks and I still hadn't heard from Buddy, or been able to find the right time to let Rayven know what the situation was between me and Bree. Every time I built up the nerve to tell her what was good, she'd bring up something in regards to our baby growing in her stomach. I told myself I hadn't come forward because I didn't want to stress her out, when in actuality, I didn't know how to break down me and Bree's complicated situation to her. No matter what I said, Bree was Buddy's baby mother and Bree and Rayven were friends, not close friends, but friends nonetheless. The fact that she and I were fucking around and crossing a lot of people was real bad. I think it was one of the reasons Bree's pussy was so good to me though. I couldn't stay from between those thick ass thighs.

One day, me and Rayven had gotten into a minor argument about her mother coming to spend the week with us in our new spot out in Queens. I left the crib mid-argument and rolled out to my crib in Manhattan. I texted Bree on the way and told her I was coming. Told her I just wanted to lay back, chill and watch a movie or something, while I gathered myself.

I was tired of arguing with Rayven. I understood she was pregnant, but it seemed like every discussion turned into an argument. I already had a million different things on my plate that my brain was trying to break down. I just needed to be in a serene space and away from the drama. Besides, she had Rabbit there with her anyway, waiting on her hand and foot.

Rabbit was a white stripper that had worked at the same strip club Rayven had, before she retired a few months back. For a white girl, Rabbit was strapped. She was built like a sista. On top of being strapped, she was fine as hell and wanted to give me some of that pussy. Every time Rayven turned her head, she was bending over in front of me. Or lifting her skirt without panties on. Sliding her fingers into her pink twat and sliding them under my nose.

She had a thing for me and Rayven knew it. I didn't understand why she allowed her to stay in our home with us, but she did, and it was one of the worst temptations I'd ever had to undergo as a man. Along with Rabbit, there were two other strippers in our inner circle. All of them were bad, and ready to be smashed in the worst way. At least, that's how I felt.

Rabbit had been essential in me getting my footing in New York. She'd been able to get the mayor of the city, Jeffery Grant, wrapped around her finger. In the process of them doing their thing, she'd taken a bunch of photos and gotten a lot of info on the mayor. And, with the help of one of Rayven's friends, we were using all of the compiled information to blackmail him. Blackmailing him had led to a lot of power and drugs and eventually, money for me. The only down side was that with the power and drugs, he expected me to destroy my own people. The more I destroyed them, the higher he promised to take me in the game.

Bree pulled open the door and stood on bare feet, dressed in a short, red lace nightgown, that came just below her crotch. She had a sly smile on her face. Her perfume was rich. It got to me right away, arousing me.

"Somebody been missing me?" she asked, stepping forward and wrapping her arms around my neck.

I slid my hands around her waist and cupped her juicy, brown, fluffy ass cheeks. They felt like hot pillows in my hands. I massaged them and sucked all over her forbidden lips. Backed her into the condo, tonguing her down.

# Rise to Power 2

"Hell yeah, I missed you, lil mama." I picked her up. She wrapped her legs around my waist and continued to tongue me down, moaning into my mouth.

I felt my dick getting harder and harder. Her breath smelled and tasted like Doublemint gum. There was nothing like a woman with fresh breath to me. It was attractive. I was a stickler for keeping my own breath fresh and clean at all times.

I crashed into the wall with her and slid my hand into her crack, nudging her panties to the side so I could play in her slit from the back, while I held her in the air. It felt wet and slimy. The lips were thick and rubbery. Her little hole was tight and running with juices. She sucked on my neck.

"I been missing you too, Kaleb. You ain't been over here in a whole week. What are you doing to me?" she whimpered and licked along my neck.

I knelt and laid her on the floor right in front of the door. Opened her thick thighs wide and sniffed her pussy with my nose right on the hole. Then, opened the lips and licked up and down, trailing my tongue around her clitoris over and over again, before sucking it into my mouth like oysters.

"Uh! Kaleb! You better stop before I wake up Breeyonna," she gasped, arching her back.

I licked the crease in the back of her legs, then down to the crack of her ass, opening the cheeks and sliding my tongue into her anus with no problem. This got her to shaking. She dug her nails into the back of my arms. Her knees were pressed to her chest. Bussed wide open for me to do my thing. The pink from between her lips looked bright, in contrast to her dark-brown sex lips. It looked so fucking good. I could smell her already. My dick beat against my stomach in anticipation for her vagina that was oozing her clear milk. I slurped it up loudly and swallowed, tasting her on my tongue, along with her lip gloss. I placed my nose over her hole again and sniffed hard. Licked along the crease, sucked the right lip into my mouth and then the left, while I kept her labia peeled all the way open.

"Kaleb. Kaleb. Come up here, baby, and let me kiss you. I just need you to hold me. Please," she whimpered.

I smushed her lips together and sucked them into my mouth. Pulled backward, then slid my tongue in between them, before opening her wide. Her crinkle came into view, more of her clear juice slid out of her. Her clitoris stood up like a mini pink penis. I flicked it with my tongue and sucked on it, teasing it, twirling my tongue all around it over and over again.

She laid back and covered her face with her hands. Screamed into them. Arched her back, and jerked twice, cumming in three squirts, bucking from the floor. Her thick thighs jiggled. I rubbed my face all in her cream. Kissed her right on the center of her pussy.

"Kaleb. Baby. Please fuck me now. Fuck me. Please."

I flipped her onto her stomach and opened her fluffy ass cheeks. Laid my face in between them, licking up and down her groove. She tasted a bit salty, but smelled like Prada perfume. Her hand slid under her body. Her fingers pinching her erect clit.

She humped into her hand while I slobbed into her ass, fucking it with my tongue. Every time I fucked forward, my face landed on her soft ass cheeks, making them jiggle like Jell-O.

"Play wit that pussy, baby. Cum for daddy. Cum for daddy right now." I attacked her clit again. Flicked my tongue from side to side, then in circles.

Her fingers went crazy between her legs. She humped the carpet harder and faster. Moaning loudly. Trying her best to look back at me. "Kaleb. I'm finna cum again.

Damn. You always doing me like this. You always fucking me over," she moaned at the top of her lungs.

I wrapped my lips around her clit again, this time sucking as if it were a nipple and I was a starving baby. I could feel her juices dripping off of my cheek. Some of it ran down the side of my face and into my ear canal.

"Uh! Uh! Uh! Kaleb! Fuck, baby! I'm cumming!" she screamed.

I continued to attack. Riding the wave of her orgasm with my teeth and tongue until she was kicking me away, with passionate tears running down her face. I pulled her leg and brought her back to me. Knelt on the side of her and placed my hard dick right on her lips.

"Suck daddy, baby. Come on." Wrapped my fingers in her hair.

She pulled back the skin and sucked me into her mouth. Then, her head was a blur in my lap. Loud nasty noises came from her lips, as she tried her best to deep throat me with her eyes closed. Her jaws hollowed out. She gagged every five sucks or so, and it drove me crazy. I humped forward and groaned in the back of my throat. Her scent was in the air. The fan placed in the window blew directly on her from the back, lighting the living room up. I couldn't wait to get in that fat pussy. Every time I did, I felt some type of way.

There was the sound of the door opening somewhere down the hall. Then, I heard Breeyonna's voice, calling for Bree. "Mama? Mama! Where are you?" she cried and sounded as if she were getting closer.

Bree turned up her sucking. She got to sucking me so fast that her gagging got louder. She pumped me with her fist and slobbered all over my pole. It dripped to the carpet.

I pushed her away and squeezed my dick in my hand, stroking it up and down. "Hurry up and go put her back to sleep. I need to fuck that pussy hard."

She nodded and stood up. My hand went between her legs. My two fingers slid all the way up her box and back out. I sucked them into my mouth and watched her pull her gown down around her lower region, before rushing into the hallway to catch her daughter before she busted us. "Come on, baby. It's okay. Let

Mama put you back to bed. Okay, honey?"

I stood there beating my meat, thinking about how her pussy looked in my mind's eye. The way the cum shot out of it and into my face, I couldn't wait to hit that pussy hard. I was yearning for it.

She didn't return until ten minutes later. Came and dropped in front of me. The big screen television played on in the background, while she slid me back into her mouth, slurping at full speed while she fingered herself slowly. Her pussy lips opened and closed around her two probing fingers.

My eyes rolled into the back of my head. I humped into her mouth, clenching my teeth and grabbed a handful of her hair, pumping my hips faster and faster. "Uh! Bree, I'm 'bout to cum, shorty. I'm 'bout to cum. Where you want it? Hurry up!"

In response, she gripped my dick with her right fist and took it all the way to the back of her throat, while her fist pumped it up and down. Stopped, slid up and sucked on the head hungrily, sucking like a vacuum cleaner. I jerked and spasmed. Tightened my grip in her hair and came hard. My toes curling. Her fist beat up and down it at full speed. She sucked me through my orgasm and didn't stop until my dick was harder than before.

She rolled over and laid on her stomach, then slowly rose with her ass in the air. Pulled her cheeks apart, and opened her pussy with two fingers, exposing her wet gap. I almost broke my neck getting behind her. I ran my dick head up and down her crease, soaking up the juices. Then on its own accord, my dick slipped into her box, falling deep into her womb. "Uh! Fuck, Bree! Fuck, boo, this pussy so hot! Damn, ma."

She threw her ass back hard, engulfing me. The meat shook, along with her thighs, then she was popping in my lap. Her fingernails dug into the carpet. She looked over her shoulder at me, with her mouth wide open. "Fuck me, Kaleb. Hit this! Hit it! Hit it! Ooh, daddy. Fuck it. Fuck it. Fuck me hard, daddy! Yes. Yes. Yes. Ooh! Fuck yes!" She lowered her head and got to really twerking like a champion. That big booty slammed into my lap and knocked me back just a bit.

I had to grab her waist, then her hips, and attack her ass back with my sword. Plunging harder and harder. Smacking her ass cheeks like she did something wrong.

"Huh! Kaleb. Don't spank me, baby. Don't spank me. I can't handle it. Aw, fuck you." She looked back at me and ran her tongue all around her juicy lips. She looked so fucking good that I was on the verge of cumming already.

*Smack. Smack. Smack.*

My open hand crashed into her meaty ass cheeks, while I long stroked her from the back like an animal.

Her juices ran down her thighs. It sounded like somebody was in the room smacking on their gum extra loud. It was so wet that my dick was shooting in and out of her in a blur. It felt so good. That forbidden pussy was so good. I knew it was wrong, but that's what made it feel so right.

"I'm finna cum, Kaleb. I'm finna cum. Put yo thumb in my booty. Put it in there. Hurry up." She moaned and laid her face on the carpet, opening her knees further apart.

I sucked my thumb in my mouth and then forced it into her back door, running it in and out while I fucked her as hard and as fast as I could. I was breathing hard. My dick head was tingling, my muscles were tensing up. My chest jumping. I gripped her hips more firmly and gave her everything I had, before I felt my nut shoot up to my stomach, then down to my piece, and out of me in big globs. "Uh. Uh. Fuck, shorty. Uh." My abs locked up.

She continued to slam backward, milking me, thirsty for my semen. The harder she slammed, the better it felt. Until finally, her assault slowed. She leaned all the way forward, collapsing on her stomach. My thumb popped out of her booty. "Damn, Kaleb. You always gotta do too much," she whimpered and turned onto her back. Reached out for me, opening her thighs wide. Her pussy was open a hint. The lips looked greasy and wrinkled. The pink shined bright in the center of them.

I fell between her legs and guided myself back into her furnace. Stroking that pussy nice and slow, while I kissed and sucked all over her lips. She rubbed up and down my back. She threatened to scratch it up with her nails. They scratched along my waistline. Her thighs were opened wide.

"I can't get enough of this pussy, Bree. This shit so good." I got down on one elbow and rolled my back. Long stroking her in slow motion. I could smell our scent in the air now. We were lighting that living room up. The fan blew on my back and it felt good. I licked all over her sweaty neck, before finding her lips again. Rolled onto my back and let her get up there. She pulled her gown along her waist again, then started to ride me nice and slow. Her face going through transformations.

"Kaleb. I'm hooked on you, baby. I swear to God, I am. I don't know what I'm about to do, but I'm sick right now. Un." She placed her hands on my chest and popped forward, making me sink deep into her body. Her heat engulfing me. I could feel her juices seeping out of her and down to my ass crack, feeling weird.

"Yo, it's good. Fuck, shorty." I humped from the carpet to dig deeper into that pussy. "We gon' figure shit out."

# Rise to Power 2

She bit into my neck and started to ride me with speed. Her back popped. Titties were squished to my chest. The nipples were rock hard, letting me know that she was overly aroused. I held that round ass and guided her to ride as hard as she could. The whole way, she moaned loudly and stuck her tongue into my ear canal.

T.J. Edwards

## Chapter 3

I got a call from Buddy out of the blue, two weeks later. I was walking around a building Rayven was thinking of turning into her own strip club. The building had been condemned six months back, and one of Rayven's connects had put her up on the property that needed about twenty thousand dollars' worth of repairs. It was smack dead in the heart of Brooklyn, right across from the Wall Street Pier. Rayven had been telling me she already had fifteen bad strippers lined up to work in the club. Strippers she'd recruited right from the Harlem River House Projects. I had been able to browse over a few of them and from what I saw, she was set to take over the game sooner or later. I dug her vision and knew I had to get a head start on putting together some of my own dreams into fruition.

Since I hadn't heard from Buddy in a while, I was on high alert. I was worried somebody had him snatched up and left in a sticky position. That they may have been using him to get me to come through, so I was ready for the worst of the worst. I wound up meeting him at a grocery store, right outside of Marcus Garvey Park. He was laid back in a red Chevy Corsica. I rolled alongside of his whip in my Benz truck and tapped the horn, looking at all of my mirrors in expectation of the unknown attack. Like I said before, I hadn't heard from the homie in weeks, there was no telling what had taken place in that amount of time. The last time I'd actually seen him, he'd had a double barrel shotgun under his chin.

He jumped out of the Corsica and jogged over to my truck and opened the passenger's door, slumping down low in the seats. The first thing I smelled was the scent of cigarettes on him. The stench made my stomach turn. Next was his breath. He was breathing heavy from jogging over to my truck. His mouth was wide open, trying to inhale as much air as possible. It was horrible. He had a black hoodie on, covering his head. He also wore black jeans and Timbs.

I had my hand on the handle of my nine millimeter, ready for whatever was to come, feeling like something was up. "Yo, where the fuck you been at, kid? You ain't answered none of your phones. You ain't been on social media. What's good?" I asked, looking all around the grocery store parking lot. It was twelve in the afternoon, bright and sunny out. It felt like it was at least eighty degrees outside. I'd already passed a few females pushing strollers, with small shorts on, all up in their asses. It looked like it was going to be a good day. But, I knew that depended on the next words that would come out of Buddy's mouth.

"Yo, it's over, kid. I ain't playing no more. I'm making muhfuckas feel my pain. It's killing season, Blood. Word up," he said and wiped his mouth. I noted his knuckles were ashy. The sleeves of his hoodie were stained with blood.

"What the fuck are you talking about, kid? The last time I saw you, that fool Gorilla had a shotgun pressed under your chin. That was before them dread heads tried to ice all our asses. In case you're wondering, I was able to save Bree. Barely, but she's alive." I looked him over closely.

He lowered himself in my seat. "That's what's up. Now peep, what I'm talking about. Them dread heads is out for blood, son. I'm talking they looking to murder us anywhere they catch us. I ain't going, son, I got my niggas up here from New Orleans, and we hunting these dread niggas and cutting their heads off. Word is bond. It's killing season. I already fucked that Gorilla nigga over. Let's roll out. I got some shit I wanna show you."

Now I was starting to smell his body odor. Buddy smelled like he hadn't had a bath in at least two weeks. I could smell every major body part on him, and they were banging like Blood and Crips. Straight up.

28

# Rise to Power 2

"Ain't that your car over there? What we gon' do, just leave it?" I asked, pointing at his car with my head.

"Fuck that whip, let's get up out of here. I don't know if I'm being followed or what. Head to the Bronx, son. I'll guide you once we get there," he said, sitting up only to peek out of the window. Then, he slid back down after making sure the coast was clear. He adjusted the guns in his waistband. I could see their chrome handles.

I drove out of the parking space, and got on to the busy street, before jumping on the expressway. "Son, when was the last time you washed ya ass? Yo, you smell real foul right now. Like funk and all that shit, word up." I lowered the window on his side and sprayed some of my car freshener in the vents. Turned the air conditioner on low. I needed some kind of relief. I hated the smell of men, I didn't care who they were.

"I'm in kill mode right now, Kaleb. And fucking wit this shit." He rolled back his right arm sleeve, and to show me that his entire arm was full of track marks. I'm on that demon, Blood. I keep that shit in my system so I can think like these niggas. Hunt 'em down and make 'em pay. Yo, if I can't kill two a day, then something is wrong. They're everywhere. They got me all outside of my body. Word up." He closed his eyes, then popped them open, very wide.

"Yo, I don't know that you're talking about, but your daughter been asking about you. So has Bree." I lied about the last part, but I felt he needed to hear some form of encouragement. By the way he was looking and smelling, I knew he didn't have a chance with Bree anymore. She was one of those real clean females and very keen on scents, like myself. Buddy was smelling so bad I could taste him from a distance. Not only that, but he had this full beard that had all kinds of lint and shit in it. Son looked horrible. I had to blame it on the heroin because I had never seen him so gross before, or smelling so bad, prior to the drug usage.

"Yo, I wanna appreciate you for holding them down, Kaleb. I owe you my life, kid, fa real. If it wasn't for you, I could have lost the love of my life and possibly even my little girl. You a real nigga. That's why I'll kill for you in a heartbeat." He sat all the way up in the seat and pulled his seat belt around his body. "Twelve be all over the Bronx now, kid. They be pulling niggas over that ain't wearing them seat belts, we don't need that right now. I got some shit I wanna show you. I'ma about to blow ya mind. That's my word." He nodded and sucked his teeth.

I mugged him for a second, wanting to ask questions, but decided against it. I didn't know if he was leading me into a trap or what, but if that was the case then he had me right where he wanted me, because I was still so mentally fucked up from him calling me a good nigga, when I felt like I was the furthest from it. I knew I was bogus for smashing his baby mother, especially with his kid in the house, but I couldn't get enough of her body, and I didn't know if I ever would. I had to let the homie know what was good. But, I didn't think this was the right time.

"Yo, pull around to the alley, and roll until I tell you to stop. I'ma have you park your truck in the garage, that way the base heads out here won't strip ya shits. They all over, kid, word up. I ain't trying to be knocking their shits loose like I am these dread heads."

I followed his directives once I got into the alley. We found a garage about halfway down. I pulled my truck into it and got out. It was pitch dark inside. It smelled stale, and like garbage. Right on the side of the garage was a big dumpster, overflowing with garbage. It smelled so bad, I had to pinch my nose.

"Yo, come on," Buddy said, waving me to follow him.

## Rise to Power 2

He walked with a rapid pace, almost a short jog, and I made sure that I kept up. We went about twenty yards up the alley, then into the back of a brownstone that he had the key to. Once in, we jogged up the steps, until we got to the very top flight. Along the way, we passed more than one base head in the hallway. They were either shooting up their dope sitting on the steps, or nodding already, scratching themselves like crazy. All of them had crazy stenches that were unbearable. After going past them, we made it to the door.

Buddy pulled a key out of his pocket and put it into the lock. "Yo, it's killing season, Blood. You finna see what I'm talking about." He opened the door and pushed it in with his shoulder.

As soon as he did, the aroma of spoiled bologna, mixed with spoiled milk hit my nostrils hard. There was a gust of heat that poured out of the apartment, along with the smells. Then, a bunch of flies flew out of it, and into my face. I fanned them away. I had never seen flies so big in my life. Buddy opened the door all the way, and stepped to the side for me to enter. He had a big smile on his face, as I walked past him and inside, on the verge of puking all over the dirty carpet. Roaches were all over the walls. And, I made out at least five rats that ran across the floor.

"Yo, what the fuck is that smell, Blood?" Re-pinched my nose again and hated to even breathe through my mouth.

He took a deep breath, and exhaled slowly. "That's the smell of war, my nigga. Word up. And it smells so good." He laughed and closed the door, then waved me to follow him once again.

I was tired of following him, because it seemed like every time I did, the conditions of things got even worse. I didn't know how much more I could really physically take. We strolled through the small apartment. There was somebody downstairs directly under his place, banging their music loud. It sounded like some kind of Reggae-ton. The beat was hitting so hard on it that I could feel the vibrations in my Jordans.

"Yo, check this out, kid. This about to blow ya wig back," Buddy said, standing in front of one of the room doors, before twisting the knob and pushing it inward. He stepped inside and directly onto a dead body. Kicked it out of the way. "Get yo bitch ass out the way, nigga." The body flipped onto its back to reveal the face had been slashed over what looked like a hundred times. The eyes were wide open, and unseeing.

I looked further into the room and had to cover my mouth from being in shock and awe. There had to be about ten bodies inside the room. All of them either had bullet holes inside of them, or their throats had been slit multiple times. Buddy walked over to one of the bodies and grabbed it by the dreads.

"Yo, this what the fuck I'm talking about, son. You see this slit in Blood's neck? I did this shit wit my katana. Cut all into his bone and everything." He pulled the head back so I could see the deep gash in the throat. It looked like an open mouth. Blood oozed out of it and ran down the dread head's collar bone. There were roaches and rats crawling all over the dead bodies. Flies whizzed through the air and landed on one corpse after the next. Maggots crawled out of a few of their noses. It was a sick sight to see, and the smell was even worst.

"Yo, what the fuck you done did, kid? What, you just snatching up dread heads and whacking they bitch ass or what?" I looked around in amazement, still couldn't believe my eyes.

"Yo, they tried to burn my baby mother, and my right-hand man's alive, son. It's all over the city that me and you iced them Jamaican bitches on the docks, when you know it was that nigga, Sheek. The gods don't get down like that, nah' mean? But fuck it, if they want war, we gon' check into that shit like a hotel, word up. I got my people from New Orleans mounted up at my duck off in Brooklyn. Kid, they Blood bound, Blood thirsty, and Blood certified. Nah' mean?" He sniffed loudly and kicked one of the dead bodies in the face so hard, one of the rats that was gnawing on its face flew into the wall and its small head bussed wide open. Blood squirt from it. His little feet were running, even though he was laid on its side.

"Yo, so why the fuck you just leaving the bodies here? These bitches supposed to be in the bottom of the Harbor or something. We don't get down like this. This is hot. You done lost yo muthafucking mind, Blood, straight up."

He jerked his head backward. "Aw, my nigga, now you got me offended, and after I done went all out of my way to give you this present I got for you in the other room." He lowered his head, then held his hand in the air, being dramatic.

"What you got for me in the other room, kid?"

He waved at me to follow him once again. I stepped over two dead bodies, and watched the rats run over to attack the dead rat whose head Buddy had bussed against the wall. We stepped out of that room, and to the door of the next one. I could hear murmuring on the other side of the door.

Buddy took the handle and smiled. "Welcome to the next chapter of things, Blood. He twisted the knob and pushed the door open. I jumped backward and pulled my pistol out of my waistband. Inside of this room were about twenty, grimy-looking-ass, dark-skinned niggas with nappy dreads, and scowls on their faces. They mugged me as if I were the enemy, and this made me want to open fire. I ain't like their stares at all.

T.J. Edwards

I couldn't believe all of them could fit inside the room like that, but somehow, some way they had managed. They were shirtless. Covered in tattoos. Five-point stars were all over them, and colored in red. Their eyes were bloodshot, and glossy. Buddy stepped into the room with them and waved his hand through the air.

"Meet my cousins, Kaleb. These are my muthafuckin' body snatchers. They gon' stand beside us and go at these dread heads with no remorse, or regard for their lives. Kid 'nem get down just like we do." Had I not already reached out to them prior to Gorilla and his Blood niggas doing what they did, this nigga would have had me dead to rights. He made his way through the crowd of niggas until he got to the closet door. Opened it and Gorilla's body fell out, with duct tape around his mouth. Buddy looked up at me. "Ta-dah, I told you I had a gift for you. I want you to slice this nigga's ass up in front of my body snatchers, kid. Show these lil niggas how we get down out here in Harlem." He dragged Gorilla to the center of the floor.

As he came forward, the crowd of niggas moved out of the way. They had anticipating looks on their faces. They looked from Gorilla on the floor, then up to me. Buddy left him in the middle of the floor, then placed his Timb on his throat. Reached into his lower back and pulled out a katana with a serrated blade. It looked sharp and twinkled in the sunlight that shone in from outside. I took the knife and looked down at Gorilla's punk ass on the floor. Stripped the tape from his mouth. It looked as if it didn't want to come off of his top lip. I pulled it a ways away from his face, before it was freed and bounced back under his blood-ied nose.

"Long time no see, bitch-ass nigga," I said, kneeling and grabbing him by the throat aggressively. I'd hated this nigga ever since I was a little kid. He'd always been a bully, sending young niggas like me off that were forced to roll

34

under him in the gang. I choked him as hard as I could for fifteen seconds, then let his neck go.

He coughed, spitting up blood onto the side of his cheek, then started laughing. Blood painted his teeth. "Aw, tough-ass Kaleb. This right up your alley here, ain't it? Me, tied up, and in no position to defend myself. This the only way you can see me at eye level, fuck nigga. You know it too." He frowned and spit blood on to the carpet. Struggled to sit up.

"Fuck you, nigga. Yo whole life, you ain't did shit but hide behind the Blood niggas in Harlem. You one of the most shiestiest niggas in the game. Now it's time yo punk ass get taken out of your misery, word up." I tightened the handle in my hand and got ready to jam the blade deep into his face. I wanted to see this punk die in front of me. I couldn't wait to send him to the Reaper. To turn him into a corpse.

"You gon' kill me like you did all them hoes, huh? Or like you did Sheek? You ain't nothing but a low-life, back-stabbing, pussy. You lucky ya mans did all of this work for you, or else I'da stanked you, nigga. Left one in the back of yo head like I was supposed to. You can't run Harlem. I don't give a fuck if you're sucking the mayor's dick or not." He swallowed a mouth full of blood and closed his eyes. "Them Jamaicans gon' kill all of you niggas. Watch. They coming, beware of them dreads, nigga. You can't out-run 'em all. Believe that."

"Yo, Kaleb, fuck what Blood talking 'bout. Slay that nigga. Word up. Slay him and let me throw his body in the next room with the rest of our victims. It's long overdue. Word up." Gorilla looked up at me and curled his upper lip. "Nigga, fuck all of you dead men walking. I'ma take mines like a G. Blood in, Blood out. Suwoo!" He inhaled and spit a thick ass loogey right into my face. It crashed into my cheek, hot and gummy. Slid down my face and dripped off of my chin, onto the carpet in a big ass, yellowish-red puddle on the floor. I cocked back and brought the knife forward, aiming for his face, out of anger. But, he lowered his head and I wound up connecting the blade with his forehead. It crashed into it and vibrated my arm. His skin split, and blood oozed out of it.

"Yo, kill that nigga, son," Buddy urged through clenched teeth.

"Yeah, fuck nigga, kill me! Kill me, bitch!" Gorilla spit again.

This time, I jumped backward out of the way. Sliced the blade through the air, catching him across the cheek. Then swung it again, and slashed him across the other cheek. It opened wide. The sight of blood fed my fury. Before I knew it, I kicked him in the face. He fell backward and I straddled him with the knife in my hand, stabbing like crazy. I raised the knife all the way over my head, bringing it back down into the soft portions of his face. The blade sunk deep all the way to the handle. Blood popped up, splattering me, then I was stabbing again, more erratic and crazy-like. The sight of the holes appearing on his face with blood pouring out of them was doing something to me. The kill was becoming fun, and exciting.

I hated Gorilla that much. I stabbed him in the face over twenty times, then stood up and watched him squirm on the carpet. Both of his eyes had been poked out, blood leaked out of their sockets. He opened his mouth to say something, but no sound was emitted. Fell on his back, and began to shake for a full minute, then passed on. Buddy walked over to him and stomped him as hard as he could in the face. "Bitch-ass nigga. Now that's how you kill an enemy." He broke out laughing.

I held the knife in my hand, dripping with blood, looking down at him. "Yo, if these dread heads want war, then let's go at they ass, Blood. Do we even know who's calling shots for them?" I asked, looking over to Buddy.

He kicked Gorilla's dead body and stepped over him. "Some nigga by the name of Rasta Man. They say he got a spot over there in Jamaica, Queens. It shouldn't be nothing to have a sit-down with him. Just let me know when you wanna do it."

I nodded. "Soon, my nigga. Real soon. But, if this nigga ain't no longer in the picture, I say we take over and flood Harlem. Our stomping grounds. If muhfuckas don't wanna roll wit the program, then we roll over they ass like we monster trucks. Word up." I sidestepped Buddy. "I hope you niggas ain't just come up here to kill shit. I hope y'all ready to get a whole lot of money too. We about to murder shit and be burping at the same time. Nah' mean?"

They looked me over, and then turned their gaze upon Buddy. Buddy laughed. "Yo, these niggas run under me. They do what the fuck I say do. So, while me and you got an understanding, let's get one more. They don't move unless I say move. Me and you will get a game plan together, and I'll make sure that the troops follow it. You got me?" he asked, looking into my eyes, almost challenging.

I looked over his men and ran my tongue across my teeth. I saw what this was. These niggas didn't give a fuck about me. Buddy was their God. So, knowing that, it told me I had to find a way to use that knowledge for the betterment of myself. They needed to become my pawns on the board of life.

T.J. Edwards

## Chapter 4

"Nigga, that's twenty kilos of China White. It's ninety per-cent. Without any steps on it. I want twenty-five per each kilo, and that's lightweight. I'm only doing this because you're my mans and I wanna see you eating like a fat bitch on her break. Nah' mean?" I took a sip from the bottle of Moet and looked across the table.

His men stood lined up against the back wall of the basement. Their faces were covered with red rags. All I could see were their eyes, which as usual, were glossy and bloodshot. They had pistols on their waists and were dressed in tight wife beaters. Buddy picked up a kilo and sniffed the aluminum foil packaging that it came in. It was covered with Chinese writing, a series of Chinese charac-ters that I couldn't make out. "That sound like five hundred thousand dollars to me, Blood. I got half of that right now." He snapped his fingers, and one of the dudes disappeared and came back with a book bag filled with a bundle of cash. He handed it to Buddy and went back to formation.

Buddy tossed the bag to me and I looked through it. It was filled with hundreds and fifties. I would have to get home to add up the total amount, but just by the looks of it, I could tell if it was not exactly two hundred and fifty thou-sand, it was close. "Yo, this what's really good right here, boss. Word up. What's the news on that meeting with Rasta Man out there in Jamaica, Queens? You got any word back?"

Buddy placed the kilos into a suitcase and shook his head. "I'm working on it. Blood 'nem so thirsty for war that they're thinking we're on some hit 'em up type shit. What's funny is that I don't know if we are or not. I don't know if I can be in the same room with them dread heads, and not put multiple slugs in their faces. Yo, I just like killing shit now. I'm obsessed." He snickered and slid the suitcase across the floor to a heavyset, dark-skinned nigga, with a cross tattooed on his forehead. He picked it up and got back into formation.

Buddy slapped his hand on the table, startling me. I mugged the fuck out of him, wanting to curse his ass out, but, held my tongue. "Yo, what's good with that Fentanyl? That a really push me and Slime over the edge. I'm talking stupid numbers."

I nodded and took my back pack off of my shoulder, opened it and placed nine ounces of Fentanyl on the table wrapped in plastic, and then tin foil. The foil was a bright pink, with dragon faces all over the packaging. I knew for a fact this was straight from Hong Kong. I'd been alongside Jeffery Grant when he'd placed the order, and received it three days later, on the border of New York in an old hangar.

"Son, that's nine ounces. Street value two hundred thousand dollars, easy. But, for you, just give me seventy-five and we're good. I need those places in Harlem that we discussed, flooded though. I'll take care of Brooklyn. I got a few lil niggas in the Red Hook Houses that I fucks with. If we got a deal on everything, then it's good. It's time to get money." I extended my hand.

Buddy shook it and slowly a smile came across his face. "Sound good to me, Blood. It's time to eat." He pulled my arm and wound up hugging me. He still smelled real foul and by this time, I was accustomed to holding my breath whenever I came into close confines with him.

We broke our embrace fast, and I exhaled and inhaled through my mouth. "Yo, I gotta go get everything else in order. I'ma fuck wit you in a few days or so. You got my new number."

## Rise to Power 2

He nodded. "Yo, what's good with Bree and my kid? You reached out to her lately?" he asked, looking me over closely.

I felt a bit of nerves go through me. "Kid, I think a better question is when are you going to check in on her and Breeyonna? You know she's missing you like crazy. Both of them."

He lowered his head. "Yeah, I know. I can hear it in her voice on the phone. Shorty sound like she's at her wit's end, kid. But, I can't allow for her to see me like this. All strung out and shit. Track marks all over the place. Yo, I'm better than this, son, and you know it, too." He exhaled and shook his head. "Yo, when I get my chips up, then I'ma meet her on mutual terms. But for right now, I just need you to look out for her and Breeyonna. They need that extra protection. I'll keep checking in from a distance until I can get my mind right, which shouldn't be long." He stepped around the table, and into my face again. "I'm letting you know right now, Kaleb, that you're the only nigga I would ever trust around my girls, man. This is a sick ass world, all across the board. Niggas ain't shit, and everybody is out for themselves, but not you, kid. You got a big heart, always taking care of the next person. One day, I'ma be just like you. I just gotta get this cold heart shit out of me first. That's real." He pulled me in for a hug and held me tight. "I'ma get right for my girls, man. You'll see. The next time I step in front of Bree, I'ma be a new man. Word up."

I didn't know what to say to all of that, so I didn't say a word. Instead, I simply held my breath, and tried to figure out how I was going to break things off with Bree. I could see Buddy was still looney over her, and that could spell serious trouble for me down the road. I kept on seeing the room full of dead bodies out in the Bronx. I didn't want to be one of them, especially not over some pussy, when the world was so full of it. Besides, I needed to focus more on Rayven. She was four months' pregnant with my seed.

\* \* \*

As soon as I opened the door to my mother's room, she jumped out of the bed and ran into my arms. Wrapping hers around my body, and kissing me on the lips, before laying her head on my chest. "Baby, I swear it feels like I ain't seen you in years."

She hugged me tighter and took a step back, looking me in the eyes wit her gray ones that matched mines. Her hair was starting to grow back. Her face looked pure and very pretty. There was a twinkle in her eye. She appeared to be gaining her weight back as well. "Explain yourself."

Instead of doing that, I went into my jacket pocket and handed her a big box from Kay's. "Huh, Mama, this just because I was thinking about your lil fine self."

She took it and pursed her lips. "Un-huh, I guess this supposed to switch the subject, huh?" She sat on the edge of her hospital bed and opened the box. Covered her mouth with one hand, and gasped. "Oh, my God. Baby, are you serious?"

I made my way over to her. "That's eight flawless diamonds. Pink lemonade. You see how bright they shining? That's what you call perfect cut and clarity right there. Only the best for my queen, word up. I know I been neglecting you with my physical presence, but I been out there grindin'. Making sure that when you step out of here, you'll step into your own house, with a nice amount of land. I owe you at least that. You're my baby." I kissed her warm cheek and nuzzled my face into the crook of her neck, like I did when I was a little boy. I inhaled her perfume, feeling safe for a moment. This was my mother. The queen of my heart. My everything. No matter how many niggas I slumped in the streets, when it came to her, I was soft like putty. She was my life. I held her to me even more.

She closed her eyes and smiled. "Boy, you be all over me like I'm your woman or something. You gone have Rayven all kinds of jealous," she teased and handed me the bracelet so I could put it on her wrist for her.

"You are my woman. Ain't nobody gone tell me different either." I kissed her cheek again and placed my cheek against hers. Holding her. Just thankful that she was alive. She had been through so much. Previously, they were only giving her a few months to live, but after moving her to a better cancer treatment center, and getting a list of better doctors, her cancer was in remission. She looked as if she was bouncing back like a basketball. I was so thankful that I didn't know what to do.

She started laughing. "I'm your woman, huh? You just gon' take ownership of me? Ain't that something." She laughed and kissed me, before there was a knock on the door.

My sister, Destiny, stepped into the room with her book bag on her shoulder. She was a mirror image of my mother, just younger. Only thirteen years of age, and already a handful. She ran to me and jumped into my arms. "Kaleb, where have you been?" she asked, slapping my chest with a frown on her pretty face.

I kissed all over her face playfully until she started to fight me off. Even then, she kept her legs wrapped around me, and her arms wrapped around my neck. "I been working lil sis, but I'm here now, and you know I'm ready to take you shopping." I sat her back on her feet.

She pulled down her dress and ran her fingers through her hair. "You lucky you said somethin' about shopping because I was definitely about to curse you out."

"Excuse me?" my mother chimed in, mugging her.

T.J. Edwards

Destiny blushed and lowered her head. "He knows what I mean, Mama." She walked over to my mother

and hugged her frame. They were already the same height. They looked like twins, all that was missing was long, curly hair on my mother's part.

Minutes later, Rayven entered the room along with my little brother, Derez. He rushed over and hugged my mother, while Rayven waddled over to me, with her stomach sticking out of her Burberry top. Her arms slid over my shoulders. Her perfume met me before she did. "Hey, daddy. I got some great news." She kissed my lips.

I tongued her down, caressing her newly rounded ass. Pregnancy had been good to my baby. Putting extra weight in all the right places. "Oh yeah, well what good news do you have for me?" I kissed her lips again, cuffing her ass. Her back was turned away from my mother, so my mother couldn't see what I was doing. I was

conscious of that.

"I closed the deal on the club this morning and the renovations are going to start tomorrow. I'm having a team of men come out to get it right. They put a time stamp of three months before it is up and running. I also got the leases for those two KFC's you wanted me to check into. It's going to cost us seventy-five hundred every sixty days to be a part of their franchise. The buildings itself are already ours, I'll explain to you how in greater detail later. But, aren't you happy? That's a whole ass club, and two restaurants. We're on our way baby. We just have to keep investing. And, you gotta keep doing your thing with college online. I love you so much." She hugged me again, and I held her for a few seconds. I felt kind of guilty because of what was going on with me and Bree behind her back. Rayven was a real good woman. We'd never gotten an understanding in regards to being faithful to one another. But, it was clear to see she wasn't fucking around on me, now that she was

44

pregnant with our kid. So, I felt crazy.

"Yeah, boo, I feel like we're making progress, but there is so much more work to be done. Now, go over there and say what's good to my mother." I kissed her lips again, and patted her ass to nudge her along. She yelped and looked back at me, laughing.

She made her way over to my mother's bed, and Destiny came back to me and slid onto my lap. Wrapped her right arm around my neck. "When are we going to spend some alone time together, big bro? Just me and you and nobody else?" Her gray eyes searched my own. My sister was also my weakness. She reminded me so much of my mother.

"Soon, baby. Is there something you want to do in general, or are you just looking to spend some time together?"

She shrugged her shoulders. "To be honest, I just want to be around you. I never see you like that and life is so short. I miss you all the time. I'd be cool with us going out and getting a slice of pizza or something. If it takes more than a few hours. I'm thinking at least a half of day." She smiled, showing off her deep dimples. She kissed my cheek and laid her head on my shoulder. I held her for the duration of the visit. She fell asleep in my arms. I couldn't help kissing her while she slept. She was so precious and perfect to me.

Midway through the visit, Derez came over and sat beside me. "Yo, Kaleb, let me hold some cash, Dunn. I know you holding mad paper. Yo name ringing in the streets, big bruh. Word."

I had to laugh at him. He was one of those caramel-skinned pretty boys. So, to hear him talk so hood was funny to me. I did all I could to make sure my little brother and sister stayed as far away from the slums as possible. The slums of Harlem was no place for anybody, but especially not for them. I'd rather die trying to make sure their lives were set, than to give up and allow the slums to raise them. I had to be the father figure we all never had. My father was a bitch in my eyes.

"Yo, you know the rules, kid. You want some scratch out of me, you know what you gotta show me." I adjusted Destiny on my lap and pulled out a knot of hundreds and fifties. Derez dropped to one knee, unzipping his book bag. He reached inside of it and came up with a stack of papers. "First of all, here's my report card. I got all A's, and one B. Fifty per A, that should get me three hundred and fifty dollars. Then, here go seven tests I got one-hundreds on. That's another three-fifty, bringing my total to seven hundred dollars even." He smiled, with his teeth showing, and closed his eyes.

I couldn't do nothing but laugh. A deal was a deal, so I counted out seven hundred dollars and handed it to him. "I'm proud of you, lil man. You gotta bring this B up to an A, but other than that, I'm real proud of you." I hugged him from my seated position.

"Boy, he don't need all that money. He's only thirteen. What in the hell is he going to do with seven hundred dollars?" My mother asked from across the room.

Derez stood up and licked his thumb, counting over the bills. "What am I not going to do with it?" he asked, nodding his head. "I gotta stack every piece of paper I can so I can open my shoe business when I turn sixteen. Word is bond, every Jordan and LeBron that come out, I'ma have them joints for a steal. My Chinese homie already got the hook-up. His people makes most of them in their basement down in Chinatown. Yo, I'ma take over the game. Watch. Then, I'ma move to jewelry, that's where the real money is. My East Indian homeboy say his family racking in a million every six months. Tax free, because they're within their first ten years in the United States. I think that's mad dope. They be eating bundles of cash like it's burgers or somethin'." He took the seven hundred dollars and wrapped it around his other bundle of cash. He had a hefty knot. It looked close to a few thousand.

"Yo, kid, I know you don't be flashing ya chips all in the open and stuff, do you?" I asked, balancing Destiny in my lap.

"Every chance he get. He almost got into a fight with two juniors today over that money," Destiny said, with her eyes still closed. She moved her head a bit on my shoulder, then yawned, snuggling into me.

"Shut up, Destiny. Dang. You always gotta tell him everything," Derez snapped. "Yo, she lying, Kaleb. Them niggas was just hating on me, because my swag is so ter- rific. That's all. Yo, I ain't about to let nobody be bullying me and all that. I'll fight, whether I lose or win. Word." He stuffed the money into his pocket and sat beside my mother on the bed, putting his right arm around her shoulder.

""Yeah, well just be careful, Derez. It's niggas in the hood that a kill you for half of that scratch. I'ma open you a bank account. Real ballers use plastic, son, not cash. Plas- tic symbolizes credit. Credit runs the world. People only respect you for how you look on paper, not with the amount of paper you're holding, trust me on that."

"Yo, Kaleb, then do that then. Open me a bank account so I can be balling like real bosses do. If cash ain't what's happening, then make me a plastic man, word up."

"Boy, you ain't no man. You're just a kid, just like me," Destiny said, facing me and laying her head on my shoul- der, before closing her eyes back.

I held her waist and kissed her cheek again. "Yeah, and I ain't about to never let you grow up either. I hope you know that." She snickered and held me tighter.

"Derez, I'll tell you what, I'll add you to my account later today. We'll start you off at five thousand. You can keep that money and spend it on whatever you want to. I'll do this, just so you can see how it feels to be in the system. Okay?" Rayven insisted.

He stood up and hugged her tight. "Thank you, Rayven. Aw, I swear when I grow up, I'ma marry you too. Not only are you super fine, but you're about your paper too. That's hot. I'm taking you from Kaleb, I'm letting you know that right now." He kissed all over her face, while she broke out laughing.

## Chapter 5

Rayven laid on her side and pulled her blue, silk nightgown up over her golden thighs. "Daddy, you think you can taste me for a minute?" she asked, lifting her right leg to expose her naked pussy. She ran her hand between her legs and slid her middle finger into herself. Then, she flipped onto her back, pulling the gown up so far that her big pregnant belly was on display.

I was standing by the dresser, going through my phone, when it vibrated. Bree's picture popped up. I held up one finger to Rayven and stepped out of the room. She balled up her face and sat up on her elbows. I could tell she was angry.

I closed the door behind me, as I stepped into the hall-way. "What's good, ma?"

Rabbit came out of the bathroom with a towel draped around her perfect body. She looked up to me and smiled. The towel was barely able to cover the fullness of her breasts. I could make out a hint of the pink areolas. The mounds looked shiny and soft. I was sure they were fake though, even though they didn't look bad at all to me. She stepped into the guest bedroom and dropped the towel, before closing the door. Her breasts jiggled on her frame. The nipples were cherry red and engorged. Then, she closed the door.

"Kaleb, I miss you so much. Please tell me that you aren't staying over there with her all night?" Bree whined into the phone like a little girl. For some reason, it made me feel some type of way.

"Yo, I ain't been here in two days, ma. I gotta spend some time with her. Besides, me and you need to talk any-way. I think we gon' have to call it quits for a little while. That nigga, Buddy, moving up in the game and son is still nuts over you. I'd hate to have to clap my nigga over his baby mother. Nah' mean?"

Rayven stepped out of the room and into the hallway, made her way toward the living room where I was standing. "Yo, who the fuck on the phone, Kaleb? You ain't never walked out of the room when I exposed this pussy. Somethin's up." She had on a robe that was opened. Her belly poked out of it. Her breasts seemed to sit right. I wanted to suck and lick all over them. Rayven was right. I could never deny her sexy body.

"Yo, chill, ma. This just Bree on the phone. I'm trying to make sure she's good. That's all." I waved her off.

She scrunched her face, and placed her hand on her hip. "Why Buddy can't do that? She ain't your problem," Rayven retorted, rolling her eyes. She stepped closer.

I took a step back. "Kid got a plateful of shit he's trying to sort out. I'm making sure she's good, since he ain't. That's it, that's all. I'll meet you back in the room, I'll be in there in a minute." I turned my back to her. "What's good, Bree?"

"Kaleb, I miss you. I need you here with me tonight. I just want you to hold me for a few hours. I need to sniff you up. Tell Rayven to chill, it's all good."

Rayven grabbed my shoulder and turned me around to face her. "Yo, hang up the phone and tend to me. I'm the one that's pregnant, she got a whole ass baby daddy of her own out there. You're mine. My baby's father, and my husband-to-be. Did you forget that?" She wiggled her fingers in my face. The ring on her engagement finger sparkled in the light.

"Fuck that! Tell her you ain't just her baby daddy, Kaleb. You mines, too. That's right! I'm two months in. I was gon' wait to tell you when you got here, but fuck that. I'm tellin' you now. We're pregnant!" Bree yelled into the phone, before I dropped it.

# Rise to Power 2

* * *

"So, when did it start, Kaleb? And I'm letting you know right now, I expect the truth. As a woman, I can handle your truths. They may hurt me in the beginning, but at least I will be able to face them like a woman and heal over time. Whereas, a lie can destroy me. I'm already hanging on by a thread after finding out that you've been fucking her all this time behind my back. It hurts. So please, be real with me." Rayven grabbed the glass of water and sat on the bed. She crossed her thighs. The gown rose all the way to her waist.

I lowered my head. "What's crazy is that I can't even tell you exactly. Sometime late last year though, while me and Buddy were beefing with Sheek and 'nem. Son had been treating her real foul, staying out late, and neglecting home. I was hitting shorty with lil lump sums of cash here and there, paying her bills and shit to make sure she and Breeyonna was good. One day, I went over to give her five bands, and that's when shit took a turn. We got to flirting. She ain't have on many clothes, one thing led to another, and it just happened."

She held up her hand. "Before the ring, I assume?"

I nodded my head. "Yeah."

She scoffed. "How many times after the ring?" She avoided eye contact with me.

I shrugged my shoulders. "I don't know, ma, a few. Every time, I felt guilty. That's my word."

She snickered. "That's your word, huh? Oh, yeah? Well, I thought what you said when you gave me this ring was your word, but I thought wrong." She got out of the bed and tried to pull the ring off her finger. She scrunched her face, then finally got it off. Looked at it and slapped it to my chest, before turning her back to me. "Give this ring to that bitch, Kaleb. Clearly, that's who you wanna be with."

I took the ring and set it on the dresser. Then walked over to her and turned her around. "Rayven, it ain't even like that, ma. You know me and Bree had history and I guess after a while, that shit spilled over into something else. It started while you were doing your own thing, besides we never talked about how me and you were going to play things. I ain't never told you to stop doing ya thing on the side, and you ain't never told me that either, so I just assumed."

She made her way over to me wit her fists balled up. "Kaleb, I swear to God, I'll buss you in yo' mouth right now. On everything, don't come at me with that lame-ass script. Nigga, you knew what it was. You knew I wasn't fucking wit nobody unless they was hitting my pockets. You was fucking that bitch on some recreational shit. Got me helping her with her bills and all of that. Smiling in my face and shit. Me taking her daughter shopping, spending time with her, and all along you was fucking that bitch, then coming over and fucking me. Nigga, I swear I oughta swing on ya ass. Word up." She took her finger and pressed it to my forehead.

I smacked her hand away, and took a step back. "Rayven, don't play wit me. You know I don't do that whole touchy-touchy shit. We gon' talk about this like adults. Straight up."

She stepped into my face, and looked into my eyes. "Are you just fucking this bitch, or do you got feelings for her, Kaleb?"

I shook my head. "It ain't even about all that. Like I said before, you and I ain't never talked about whether we were going to be faithful to one another or not. I just assumed it was good. At least, I ain't out there fucking every random bitch that open their legs for a nigga. You feel me?"

"Hell nall, I don't feel you. Instead of you fucking some random female, you go out and fuck ya right-hand man's baby mother. A bitch we both grew up with. Shit, we just went shopping together last week and I was telling her how much I was missing you, and how I wished you were home more. All along, she was laughing at my needy ass. Laughing because she knew that every time you weren't with me, you were marinating your dick in her. That's trifling and low. I can't believe you. I wanna fight you so bad right now, I'm shaking. I swear, I never imagined that you'd do me like this. Not only am I hurt, I'm disappointed." She turned her back again, and started to mumble to herself. Her short nightgown had gotten stuck on her hip. The bottom halves of her cheeks were visible. "Do Buddy know? Huh?" She turned around to face me.

I shook my head. "Nall, and I'm trying to keep it that way. I ain't trying to fuck with her on that level. I just got caught up in the fucking side of things. I screwed up. Damn." I hung my head and started to think things over real rapid in my mind. I couldn't believe Bree was saying she was pregnant. I was praying she was just saying that to scare me. I couldn't imagine the backlash I'd have to face with Buddy. I knew for a fact we were set to go to war, and what made shit so crazy is that I felt like he had the upper hand in the moment. Kid had them hittas from New Orleans, ready to murder on command. That was scary to me. Especially because I knew he was head over heels in love with Bree. She was his heart. If she just so happened to honestly be pregnant, it was about to go down. I had to step my army up. All the way up. I needed some cutthroats on my team. Murderers. Animals. Niggas that would kill on command, like Buddy had.

Rayven snickered. "Nigga, you worried. I can see that shit all in your eyes. You're worried that when Buddy finds out you got his bitch pregnant, he gon' go bananas and start to wilding out. And, you should be. You and Bree are real foul, dude. You're lucky I love yo ass or I'd be bucking your ass down with my registered pistol right the fuck now. I promise you, I would." She laughed and sat on the bed. The hem of the nightgown traveled upward, exposing her golden thighs. They looked creamy and thick. "I should call his ass. Let him know what's good, since I can't do nothing in my current state." She smiled as if she were imagining it in her mind.

I scrunched my face. "Rayven, stay in yo muthafucking lane. Don't get to playing games with people's lives and shit. That nigga a buss his gun over that girl, just like I would over you. Now, I know you're feeling some type of way, but let me figure this shit out. I fucked up, so I'ma handle it. Keep yo muthafucking mouth shut. You understand that?" I snapped, standing over her.

"What?" She jumped up and placed her hand on her big belly. "Nigga, fuck you. I don't owe you shit. If I wanna get on my phone that I'm paying the bill for, call Buddy and tell him what's good, then that's what I'ma do. I ain't scared of you. What, you think it's sweet wit me because I'm pregnant?" She stepped into my face and pushed me so hard, I flew backward into the dresser, and bunch of her cosmetics she usually applied before bed, fell to the floor. "Fuck you, Kaleb. Let's get it."

The first thing that went through my mind was that she was pregnant, and I was in the wrong for fucking off on her behind her back. Even though she'd just pushed me into the dresser, I had to give her a pass. That I couldn't put my hands on her, while she was pregnant with my kid. So, I caught my balance and stood up. Chilled for a minute, with my nostrils flaring open and closed. My heart was beating fast, and I was getting madder and madder. But yet, I tried to calm myself as best I could. But, it wasn't easy.

Rayven's yellow face was beet red. Her balled fist went in front of her face like she was ready to throw down. "This Harlem right here, Kaleb. You gon' beat my ass, nigga, bring it." She bounced on her pretty, painted toes and moved to the center of the bedroom.

"Rayven, stop playing wit me. Go over there and sit yo ass down before I fuck you up. I'm trying real hard right now to give you a pass." I took one step backward, trying to avoid the inevitable. But, that was the problem with most chicks from Harlem. They loved to come at niggas on that fighting shit. You'd literally have to fuck them up, in order for them to get the message. I wasn't trying to go there with Rayven, but she was pushing it. I was seconds away from getting on her ass.

"You know what, shorty, I'ma leave for the night. Take a chill pill and then we gon' try this again tomorrow. I do want to apologize for doing what I did. And, I don't know how, but I'ma do all that I can to make it up to you. That's my word." I grabbed my gun out of the top drawer, put it into my pants. Then slid my feet into my black and gray AirMax 95's that offset the fit I was wearing. I needed to get out of there before I did the unthinkable.

Rayven rushed over to me, swinging wildly with her fists hitting me all in the face, and neck. I mean hard ass blows too. When I felt my teeth poke into my bottom lip, I knew something had to shake. "I know you just going to that other bitch. I know that's where you going. I ain't stupid, Kaleb. What do you take me for? I'ma kill you." She started to swing faster and faster.

I covered my head for a minute, then stood up and smacked her so hard that she fell to the floor on one knee. Blood gushed out of the opening in her lip. Tears began to spill down her cheeks almost immediately. I stood there with the open palm of my hand on fire. "I told you to calm yo ass down. Fuck. Just because I made a mistake, don't mean you about to treat me like some simp-ass nigga. This ain't that, shorty. I'll spank yo ass in this bitch. Word."

Rayven slowly got up and wiped her mouth. Held her stomach and smiled. She looked at her bloody fingers. "I got your baby inside of me, and this is what you do?" She sucked her teeth. "Okay, nigga. I see what it is. Gon' 'head. Get dressed. Go clear your mind. I'll see you when you get home." She looked at her fingers again, then back up to me. Walked into the bathroom and closed the door loudly.

I stood there looking like a damn fool. Sick. I couldn't believe I had put my hands on my baby mother. That I'd made her draw blood from her mouth. I felt like a bitch-ass nigga. Lower than scum. What type of nigga beat his pregnant woman? A bitch nigga, that's what type. I walked over to the door and knocked on it. "Rayven! Yo, open up the door, ma. Please. Let me holler at you for a minute."

"Kaleb, go handle yo bidness, Dunn. I ain't fucking wit you for a minute. I gotta get my mind right. This whole night has been a curve ball for me." I could hear the water in the sink running.

I imagined her dabbing the corners of her mouth with a towel. Wiping away blood I'd made her shed. I felt like shit.

"Ma, I'm sorry. Yo, I love you, goddess. You've always been there for me. I fucked up. I shouldn't have. Yo, why don't you come out here and get your lick back, then let's talk about all of this."

Rabbit peeked her head into the bedroom. "Do you want me to talk to her for you?" she asked, wearing a button-up that was half unbuttoned. The tanned swells of her breasts were clear and visible. Her nipples poked at the shirt. Rayven opened the door, before I could answer Rabbit. Cocked back and punched me right in the mouth, splitting both my upper and bottom lip. The hit caught me off guard and knocked me backward.

"There go my lick back. Now get the fuck out of the house! Go tend to that bitch while I get my head together!" She grabbed Rabbit by her hair and pulled her into the bathroom and slammed the door.

# T.J. Edwards

## Chapter 6

Bree sat across from me on the couch with her head lowered. She took a deep breath, and shook her noggin. On the table in front of us were five pregnancy tests, all of them were positive. Breeyonna sat on her side of the couch, playing her tablet. She looked as if she didn't have a care in the world. I loved my goddaughter. Ever since she'd been alive, I'd made sure she had been well taken care of on all fronts. Buddy rarely reached for her, even when he had bundles of cash and I always thought that was foul. But, it was small things to a giant. She was pure. I had to make sure she remained that way.

"So, what do you want me to do? The smart thing would be to get rid of it, right?" she asked in a defeated voice.

I grabbed the bottle of Patrón off of the table, and turned it up for the fifth time in an hour. I was drunk as hell. Half the bottle was gone. I couldn't feel the pain in my lips anymore. I was thankful for that. It had only been twenty-four hours since me and Rayven had gotten into our dispute, and she was real heavy on my mind. She wasn't answering any of my calls or returning my messages. On top of that, she had me blocked from her Facebook and Snapchat. I felt a bit lost. "Nah, I ain't about to have you kill my baby. I'ma be a man and do what I gotta do for all of us. We laid down and made this child together, so I'ma hold you down." I came over and sat next to her on the couch, after moving Breeyonna out of the way.

She kept right on playing her game on her tablet as if nothing even happened. Her long hair was in a bushy ponytail. She had on her pajamas and should have been in bed, but for some reason, she wanted to be all up under us.

"Then, what about Buddy? You already know when he finds out I'm pregnant, he's going to flip his lid. I can see him killing me with no hesitation. I'm so worried. I don't know what to do." She laid her head on my shoulder. Took a deep breath. "Kaleb, do you love me?"

I switched the bottle of Patrón into my right hand and put my left arm around her shoulders. "Yeah, I do. It's the type of love that tells me I gotta protect you at all costs. I want to witness your growth. I want to help you excel as much as I can. I sincerely apologize for putting this baby in you. It ain't fair. I should have been smarter than I was. That p-u-s-s-y so good though," I said, spelling it out so that Breeyonna wouldn't know what we're talking about.

She giggled and shook her head. "*We* should have made better choices. But, we still can. I don't have to have this child. Especially, since it's going to cause so much conflict. If you asked me what I wanted to do, I'd say we fix this before Buddy catches wind, or Rayven creates so much drama that I can't go anywhere in New York. She's well connected. Even got friends in high places. The last thing I'd want is to be walking somewhere, and a group of women come out of nowhere just to jump on me and kick this baby out of me. I mean, I love you and all, but, you remember what he did to Ryo when he thought him and I were screwing around. He gunned him down in damn near broad daylight. He's a loose cannon. He is going to flip his lid. It ain't worth it. I mean, at least that's how I feel. What about you?" She grabbed my hand and laid her face into the palm of it, breathing with a concerned look on her face.

I took another swallow from the bottle. A part of me wanted to agree with her. Buddy was going to be a problem. Then, there was Rayven, the love of my life. I didn't want to lose her. I loved Bree, but not like I loved Rayven. Rayven had been with me through so many things, including my mother's bout with cancer. It was because of her that I had been able to get her moved to a very prestigious hospital. She had thrust Mayor Grant into my life and placed me on the path to riches because of his plugs. She was a mastermind. Determined to conquer New York in her own way, and I wanted to be connected to her because of her drive, ambitions, and the unconditional love I had for her.

I couldn't lie, Bree was so tempting though. Every time I was in the same room with her, I just couldn't help myself. She was so alluring, and I think the fact that she was on rock bottom and needed me to pull her upward was another contributing factor. Although, I still didn't know if us bringing a child in the world while all of these things were at play was a good idea. There was already the war with the dread heads looming in the distance. But, at the same time, I was against that abortion shit, unless a woman had been raped, or somethin. I could not see myself giving her permission to murder my seed. Regard-less of the circumstances. I was a better man than that.

"Yo, honestly, I don't think it would be the smartest idea for us to bring this child into the world. I mean, you got crazy ass Buddy on the prowl. Then, like you said, Rayven ain't accustomed to taking no L's. Sooner or later, she gon' get at you, ma. I'm just keeping shit one hunnit. On top of that, it's time for you to get your goals in order. I gotta help you get to the top by any means. I think a baby, with all the drama surrounding it, will hinder you from becoming the best you that you can become. However, I'm rolling wit you whichever way you wanna go. I'm just letting you know it ain't gon' be easy if we keep it."

She bounced from the couch and started to pace. Breeyonna paused her game and looked up at her curiously. "You okay, Mama?"

Bree nodded her head. "Baby, go to your room for a little while so I can talk to Kaleb. I don't want you to hear our bad words."

Breeyonna scooted from the couch and hugged my neck. "But, I'm not sleepy, Mama. I don't want to miss my god daddy. I love him," she whimpered, hugging me tighter around the neck.

I picked her up, and carried her into the hallway, kissing her soft cheek. "It's okay, baby. I'll be here when you wake up in the morning. Me and your mother just need to talk for a little while, okay?"

She started to cry, nodding her head. "Okay, but I still don't want you to go. I love you, god daddy." I lowered her into her bed, and tucked her in.

I leaned down and kissed her forehead. "I promise that when you open those pretty brown eyes, I'ma be here, okay? I won't let you down. That's my word to you." I smiled down at her.

She looked up at me and smiled back. "Okay, but promises are supposed to never break. They are made of steel, just so you know." She did the "come here" signal wit her little finger, so I leaned down.

As soon as I was close enough, she kissed my cheek. The small gesture of affection warmed my heart. I felt kind of emotional. Ever since she'd been in existence, she'd found a way to steal pieces of me. I wondered how a child that me and Bree made together would be. If it was anything like Breeyonna, it was a child I did not want to abort. I wanted to bring them into this world and go hard for them every second of every day.

As I was tucking Breeyonna all the way in, Bree came to the door and pushed it open. "Come on, baby. We need to get some things out so I can sleep on this. Come on."

She walked away from the door, headed toward the living room. I kissed Breeyonna's forehead one more time.

Flipped on her *Frozen* nightlight and left the door open a crack. "Good night, princess. I love you, lil mama."

Back in the living room, Bree was pacing back and forth. "Why do you have to do shit like that, Kaleb? Why?" she asked, running her fingers through her hair. She looked distressed, and sick.

I was confused. "What are you talking about? What did I do now?"

"With Breeyonna, just now. I watched how you treated my daughter. How you carried her away and spoke softly to her. Reassuring her that you were hearing her out. That you would be here for her in the morning. Kissed her in the right places and comforted her little soul. I saw all of that, Kaleb. Damn you," she said, shaking her head again.

"Bree, pardon me if I'm missing something. But, I don't get it. What have I done wrong?"

"Her daddy ain't shit, Kaleb! He ain't never talked to my baby like that. He ain't never been there for her. He ain't never gave a damn, until he thought another man was doing his job. Then he acted like he wanted to step in and up to the plate. He's ridiculous. Breeyonna deserves a father like you. Somebody that will care about her. Fight for her. Take care of and comfort her. She needs you. And, I think the only way she will be able to have you consistently is if you are the father to her sibling. So now, you got me thinking about locking your ass down for those purposes. Damn you."

I slid beside her and pulled her into my arms. Rubbing her back. "Baby, it's good. You ain't gotta pull a move in order for me to be there for her, or you. That's that project shit. We're better than that. I'ma hold y'all down because my love for the both of you is real. That's my goddaughter and you're my baby. That's just what it is. I been crazy about you, just like you are about me."

She broke out of my arms and turned her back on me. "Why though, Kaleb? Why do you even care about me? I'm a single mother. I don't have a career, money, or no direction right now. I got a crazy ass baby daddy that's strung out on heroin that promises to murder any nigga that even looks at me too long. I'm not the finest woman in New York, and I don't have much to offer you. Why do you want to be here for us? Why?"

Hearing her lay her cards on the table like that attracted me to her even more. She was vulnerable, at rock bottom and I was in a position to lift her up. I needed to be her savior. Needed to put her in the game, and on her feet. It was imperative that I did so, because I didn't like seeing her hurting, or a dependent. She was a queen in my eyes. And a queen was supposed to sit high upon a throne of greatness. A throne that I would provide for her. It was time to get moving.

"Yo, I ain't going nowhere. I know you ain't feeling me right now, but I'm feeling you. And I'ma hold you down. We gone do this shit together. You ain't about to be some statistic. Poor and left behind in the ghettos of Harlem with two children with different fathers, and not a pot to piss in. Over my dead body. I got you." I turned her around and pulled her to me. I ran my hands over that big ass booty. Squeezing that soft thang. I massaged the cheeks and kissed her lips. "I got you, baby. We gone start from the bottom and place you on top where you belong. But it's time you embrace that you are a queen. Your current circumstances should never affect who you are to become. You are special." I sucked all over her juicy lips.

She moaned into my mouth and tongued me down. Stepped forward into my hard piece that was pointed down my leg. Trapped it between her thighs and squeezed it. "Kaleb, I want you to fuck me right now. You hear me?" she moaned, tonguing me down.

# Rise to Power 2

My hands were already under her skirt. Pushing her thong to the side and playing over her bald kitty lips. They were wet. I searched and found the hole. Slid my middle finger into it and worked it in and out. Digging as deep as I could. "I want some of this pussy too, Bree. I'm feening for you, ma." I sucked her neck. Her moans got louder.

She leaned her head to the side. "You can have this pussy whenever you want it, Kaleb. It's yours, daddy. You know it's yours." She backed up on my hand and spread her pretty feet apart so I could dig deeper into her body. My fingers were running in and out of her at full speed. They were sloppy wet, drenched in her juices. I could hear the swishing sound coming from between her legs.

"Un. Kaleb. What you about to do to me?" I pushed her over the arm of the couch and yanked that skirt up over her hips. Her dark caramel ass popped into view and it jiggled at me. Then, my tongue was licking all over it. Kissing the light stretch marks that were barely visible. The ones that confirmed to me that her ass was real. I licked up and down her thick thighs. Tasting her. I could smell her perfume. For some reason, because of where I was, it smelled as if it were mixed with fire. It was intoxicating. I trapped her pussy lips within my mouth, and sucked hard on them. "Uh, Kaleb. Don't start this shit, daddy. Don't start. I just want you to fuck me. Don't tease me. Please don't tease me."

She looked over her shoulder at me, licking her juicy lips. Reached under her belly and held her pussy lips open for me. I licked up and down her slit, and all over her fingers, licking the juices off of them. And she was oozing so much, it looked like she was peeing. That was one thing about Bree. When her pussy got wet, it got real wet. My neck was already drenched in her fluids, and I was trying to swallow everything that came out of her with little success. I loved eating her pussy. "Baby, I'ma bout to make you cum in my mouth. Cum on this tongue, boo. Now. Come on me, boo. Please," I begged, needing to taste her badly.

She pinched her clit, while I attacked it with my tongue. I fingered her hole and sucked hard. Raised my hand and slammed it down hard on her ass. She screamed, threw her head back and came all over my lips. Bucking back into me. Shaking, nearly falling over the arm of the couch. My tongue traveled up and down her slit. Then stopped to pull on her clit with my lips. Sucking hard, praying for more of her juices.

She fell to the floor, turned onto her back, rubbing her pussy in a circular motion with all four of her fingers humping into them. "You always get me like this. You always make me play wit myself like this. Uh, fuck!" She slid two fingers into her pretty pussy and got to going to town.

Her cream oozed out of her hole, fizzed around her assaulting fingers, and slid down into the crevice of her ass crack. I fell to my knees and hurried across the carpet. Grabbed the backs of her knees and pushed them upward until her kneecaps were planted against her shoulders. Her pussy bussed wide open, exposing her pink. I licked in between her crack, then all the way down into her asshole. Ran my tongue in and out of it. Swallowed her juices, then sucked her clit into my mouth again, while my tongue ran circles around her jewel. Her scent was heavy now. It felt hot between her legs. My dick dragged against the carpet, throbbing and jumping in my pants. I was feening for some sort of relief. I wanted to fuck her as hard as I could, knew I was moments away from doing so.

She pulled the straps on her blouse down to expose her breasts. Both nipples were erect, and sticking up an inch from her mounds. She pulled on them, wet her fingers, and trailed them in circles, before pinching them hard, and yelping. "Kaleb. Get yo ass up here and dick me down. I need that Harlem shit. I need that Harlem shit, daddy. I'm so fucking serious," she gasped, out of breath.

I smushed her sex lips together and a clear droplet of juice seeped out of her hole. I slurped it up. Then stood on my knees, pumping my dick while I looked between her thick thighs. "Touch that pussy, baby. Let me see you play wit it while you look at yo daddy lusting all over yo lil thick ass." I rubbed her pussy, gathered some juices and trailed my thumb around the head of my piece. It sent chills through me.

She laid back on one elbow and opened her thighs wider. Ran her fingers into her crack, opened the lips, then slid her middle finger into herself. Sucked it into her mouth. "Um, daddy. This how I used to play wit my pussy when I was a little girl. Watch me." She pinched her clit, smelled her fingers. Sucked them back into her mouth, moaning around them. Then placed them back between her legs, opening and closing her lips. One second her pink would be exposed. Then the lips were smushed together. Her ass bounced up from the carpet and slammed back down hard. Jiggling. Her juicy thighs shook as well. I watched her cream spurt out, and it was too much for me.

I rushed between her legs and forced them apart even more. I lined myself up, and slammed into her. Grabbed her right leg and tossed it on to my shoulders. Then got to long stroking that hot pussy like a savage. Digging deep, while my abs crashed into her stomach.

"Un! Un! Uh! Uhf, Kaleb! Slow! Down I You fucking me! You fucking me so hard! Shit! Shit! Shit! Daddy! I thought! Uh! Fuck! That you loved me! Shit!" My dick slammed into her hot pocket. My balls crashed into her ass before I cocked back and slammed him home again.

Her pussy got to making all kinds of forbidden noises. Sucking at me. Trying to trap me inside at the same time it tried to push me out. It was tight. The walls felt thick, with ridges. I couldn't help groaning against her shoulders. Almost whimpering. She was so damn strapped and that pussy was so forbidden, it could get me killed. I was murdering that killer pussy while she dug her nails into my back, and screamed in my ear. She was vulnerable. I felt like she needed me. And because she did I felt like I had use. I felt as if I had worth. My feelings for her began to develop, every time I thought about where I could take her in the game. I knew I wanted her by my side. Knew I wanted to make her a queen. I forced her onto her side, grabbed her left thigh, cuffed it, and started to really dick that pussy. Hitting her bottom. It oozed all over me. My hips was dripping because of her.

"I'm finna cum in this pussy, baby. I'm finna cum. Daddy finna put his nut all in you. Tell me you ready," I growled. "Tell me."

She fucked back into my lap. Her hair was all over her face. Sweat drooled down her neck, and it didn't stop me from licking it up while I fucked her harder and harder. "Daddy, I'm cumming too. I'm cumming too. Aw. Fuck. I need you. I swear I need you. Cum in yo baby. Shit!" She slammed back as hard as she could, and closed her eyes. Using the bottom of the couch for leverage. Her ass shook every time it crashed into my lap. This made me bite her on the neck and growl like a pitbull. My body tensed up. My balls shot into me, and the next thing I knew, I was cumming in jerks. Nut flew out of my head like Elmer's glue. Hitting her walls, and the deepest regions of her vagina. She shook under me. Grabbed a handful of the carpet and came over my pile driver, before I collapsed on that ass, breathing hard.

# Chapter 7

I don't know how it happened, but two weeks later, Buddy wound up getting locked up in New Jersey. Twelve had pulled him and a few of his New Orleans homies over, and found the car loaded with handguns and one assault rifle. His bail was a hundred thousand. And, he got word to me through Rayven that he needed me to come through for him. The hundred thousand wasn't really a problem, but there was no way I could walk into any precinct in New Jersey with one hundred bands and not expect them to get the feds involved, so I thought it was in my best interest to get a bail bondsman, which I did. Buddy got popped off on a Thursday, and I didn't find a bail bondsman until Friday afternoon.

By the time we got all of the money and shit squared away, it was too late for us to go and get him out, so we had to wait until Monday morning. Instead of keeping the homie in the blind, I decided to roll out and visit him in the county. I got there early Saturday morning. It was over eighty degrees by ten o'clock that morning, which sucked for me. The homie had begged for me to bring Bree along with me, and me and her argued for a whole hour before she agreed. We sat behind the glass for fifteen minutes be-fore Buddy even showed up.

Bree held my hand under the small table. "I don't want to be here, Kaleb. I don't give a fuck about this nigga no more. I'm in love with you. You're my life now. Fuck him," she spat, and leaned in to kiss me. I moved my face out of the way just in time.

The correctional officer opened the big metal door on the other side and the next thing I knew, we were looking at Buddy. He made his way to his assigned seat on the other side of the glass, and sat with a big smile on his face. He looked ten pounds skinnier then when I'd seen him last. His eyes were bloodshot. He looked sick. I could tell he was feening for a fix.

I let Bree's hand go, when I saw him pick up the phone. I grabbed the one on our side, and wiped it clean with Purell, then placed it to my ear. "What it do, Blood?"

He nodded. "Yo, why the fuck am I still in here, kid? A hunnit bands is peanuts to you now, I'm sure of that. What gives?"

I scoffed. "I ain't get you a bail bondsman until late yesterday. I paid Blood, and everything is everything, but they hollering ain't shit moving until Monday, so that's what it is. I handled my end as fast as I could. You can express some sort of gratitude too, kid. Damn, nigga."

He ran his good hand over his face. "Yo, that's my bad. You're right. I appreciate you for moving as fast as you did. I know you got a lot of shit on yo plate too. My family included." He looked past my shoulder and over to Bree. She was sitting beside me with her head down. Under the small divider, her fingers were clasped around my pinkie. I could tell she was both angry and annoyed at being there. "What's good wit my Missus? She been asking about me or what?" he asked, smiling.

I lowered the phone from my ear and handed it to her. "Yo, son wanna know what's good. Holler at him for a minute and keep that shit classy. Nah' mean?" I moved from the stool and let her switch places with me.

She took a deep breath, before she put the phone to her ear. "What's up, Buddy? What you wanna talk to me about?" she asked in a lazy-like voice.

I couldn't hear what Buddy was saying on the other side of the glass, so I took my time to look over the small visiting area. There was a row of metal stools, most of them were occupied by visitors that had phones in their hands. There were a few other people sitting on the extra stools like I was. One female in particular acted as if she couldn't take her eyes off of me. She was light-skinned, with electric green eyes. She had long curly hair, and juicy lips. Her thighs were crossed, but from what I could see they were plump. On her feet were a pair of red-bottomed heels. She waved and smiled. I looked off and acted like I hadn't seen that. Turned back to the glass where Buddy was all frowned up, looking like he wanted to buss through the glass.

Bree took a few deep breaths and pursed her lips. "Buddy, why are you getting so angry? I should be the one that is angry at you, because you ain't been doing nothing for Breeyonna. And, I know you be having money, because a few of my girls that are dealing with a couple niggas in your crew, say you the man now. So, what's good?"

I could hear the bass from Buddy snapping on the other side. He punched the glass over and over. Bree held the phone away from her ear and closed her eyes. Shook her head, then continued to listen to the rant he was going in on her with.

Meanwhile, the redbone down the way still couldn't take her eyes off of me. She did the "come here" signal with her finger. Since I didn't feel like hearing them argue for the next ten minutes, I got up, and met her halfway.

She held out her hand. "Your name is Kaleb, am I right?" Her green eyes ran all over me. She even took a slight step back and looked me up and down. I was trying to place her face. But, she didn't look familiar to me at all.

"Yeah, and how might you know that?"

"You went to Malcolm X Middle School, over in Harlem. You were in Mrs. Smith's class. In fifth grade, you sat in the third row from the door. You see, I remember, because you were the first boy that made me feel weird between my little legs as a kid. I think it had a lot to do with those gray eyes. That and all of the girls used to be all over you."

I shook my head. "I'm so sorry, but I don't remember you at all. And, I wish I did." I looked her up and down. I could hear Bree arguing with Buddy in my background.

She smiled. "Lucky for you I got a picture." She took the Gucci purse off of her arm and went inside it, pulled out her wallet and then a fifth grade class picture. "That's you right there and this is me." She pointed to a picture of a yellow little girl with acne all over her face. She had head of curls.

"Trinity? Really? This is what you transformed into?" I asked, looking her up and down. Her Gucci dress was molded to her perfect frame like a glove. I made her twirl in a circle so I could get a back view. Even peeped her toe game, which was on point. She had the Gucci symbols on both her fingernails and toes. She looked good.

She laughed out loud. "Damn, you act like I was ugly back then or something. Was I?"

"I don't know, ma, I was in the fifth grade. You definitely ain't now though. What do you do for a living?" A woman that looked as good as she did had to have her hand in something in New York. The Apple was a city where everybody had to be on business, or the city would eat you up and spit you out. Leave yo ass in one of the many gutters that it offered as a final resting place to low lives, and people with no ambition. "I got my hand in a little bit of everything. But mostly, I'm doing real estate, and club promoting. What about you?"

"I got a few restaurants under my belt. Trying to acquire some property and figure life out as I go along. You know, just taking it one day at a time."

"You know, a man should take time out each day to map out his life. He should never roam about with no set plan of action. You are never supposed to be standing in the same position today that you were standing in yesterday. You have to think like a king. Life is too short." She smiled. "I'd like to catch up with you. Sit down, and maybe have some lunch or something. That's if Bree won't have a problem with that. She still looks good too, for the record."

As she said this, she was looking over my shoulder toward her. And of course, Bree was still arguing with Buddy. I nodded. "I'd like that. Especially because I wanna pick your brain about some things. Maybe we can help each other in some way. You never know." She took my hand again and shook it, then handed me a card with her real estate business logo and contact information on it. Turned the card around and started to write something on it. "This is my Facebook, and direct cell info. Make sure you hit me. I really wanna get to know you." She kissed my cheek, then started to walk away.

I didn't know how long Bree had been watching, but this made her jump up and head in our direction with her face balled up. "Wait a minute, who the fuck is she, Kaleb?" She acted as if she was about to bump me out of the way, until I grabbed her.

"Yo, chill, don't make a scene here. Think about Buddy's ass."

She tried to push me off of her. "Fuck Buddy. He's a dope head now. There is no saving him, but you still ain't answer my question. Who is she, and why was she all up on you like that?"

Trinity placed a tuft of her curly hair behind her ear. "Uh, hi Bree. It's me, Trinity, from fifth grade. I saw Kaleb and I just wanted to say hi, that's all. I didn't mean you no disrespect. Seriously." She extended her hand.

Bree slapped it away. "Bitch, stay yo pretty ass away from Kaleb. He's spoken for. I can tell by how you're looking at him, you're eating him up inside of your mind right now. It ain't happening. You've been warned." She rolled her eyes and grabbed me by the shirt.

## T.J. Edwards

I smacked her hand away. "Shorty, get yo ass over there and sit back down. Stop acting all crazy and shit. Come on." I led her back to Buddy's window. He was sitting at the glass with his head down, mumbling to himself.

When I picked up the phone, it smelled like Bree's Prada perfume. Bree sat down and crossed her arms with her back to the window. "Yo, why you over here mumbling to yourself and shit'?" I asked Buddy. I tried to have a slight smile on my face, but I could tell that he was sick. It was written all over his face.

"Yo, I lost her, kid, and it's murdering my soul right now. I feel less than a man. This heroin got me on the ropes, kid. I can't lose my baby, though. You know I'll kill a nigga over her ass. Word up, B. If I can't have her, then I don't want her breathing. I'm gon' tell it like it is." He slammed his hand on the ledge in front of him.

"Stop talking stupid, son. She ain't going nowhere. You just gotta get out and get your shit in order. That's all. You got two women that are looking to you to be their savior. And one isn't even a woman yet, but she will be."

"We don't need him. The only reason I came is because you made me. I gave up on you a long time ago, Buddy. You ain't nothing but a dope fiend. Fuck you!" She stood up and flipped him the bird, then stormed out of the visiting area.

The big metal blue door slammed behind her. I'd managed to hold the receiver of the phone for most of her rant. Buddy was beating on the glass, trying to get me to take my hand away so he could hear everything she was saying, but I was worried about her exposing our relationship, so I refused to roll those dice. I was smarter than that.

When I put my ear back on the phone, Buddy was snapping. "Blood, on everything I love when I get out of here, I'ma knock that bitch head off. She's fucking somebody. I can tell. She only get to acting all stupid and shit when there is another nigga in the picture. I need you to find out what's good for me. As soon as I get out of here, I'ma whack both of they ass together, Harlem style." He was talking so fast, there was spit all over the glass.

Imagining this nigga hurting Bree in any way had me vexed. I was doing all I could to not let that shit show in my face. "Buddy, you just stressing right now, but you gon' be good come Monday. Get you up out of here and get some fresh air. That's all you need. Stop talking that dumb shit though."

Buddy sucked his teeth and leaned into the glass. "Nigga, fuck what you talking about. Somebody fucking my bitch, and I ain't going. I'm locked down right now and she acting like she don't give no fuck. That means I'm dead to her, so since I'm dead to her, she gon' be dead to me. That's my word. All I need you to do is to keep looking after her and Breeyonna, until I get home. When I do, I'm icing her on day one. Matter fact, I'ma have one of my lil niggas touch bases with you tomorrow and have him handle this bitch before I even step out the door. That way, when I get out, I can have my mind focused strictly on Breeyonna. The sight of Bree with breath in her lungs ain't gone do shit but make me relapse. So, when my nigga hit you up, get back at him, aiight?" He slammed both of his hands on the table and got up, left the glass. I sat there for a long time steaming. How could any nigga put a hit on their baby mother? That was bitch shit. And on top of that, she was no longer just his baby mother. She was mine as well. It was my job to protect her. And I was going to do that by any means necessary.

* * *

When I got back to my truck, Bree was sitting in the passenger's seat with her face covered, crying her eyes out.

Tears found their way through the cracks of her fingers. I closed the door and pulled her into my embrace. "I gotta get you out of New York. Blood hollering that he want you dead. He supposed to be sending one of his hittas at you tomorrow, but you already know what's finna happen with that."

She sat back in her seat, and wiped tears from her cheeks. "I'm so tired of him, Kaleb. I'm so tired of being trapped by that nothing-ass man. If the only way for me to escape him is death, then so be it. I swear, I don't even care no more." She covered her face again.

"Yo, so you just gon' roll over and die? This how you about to get down? This is the real you? The woman who's carrying my seed?" I was disgusted. Felt like snapping out on her and would have if I hadn't heard her crying harder. I sat there for a second, looking out onto the sunny day. My window was rolled down a crack and there was a nice breeze coming through the window. I sat back in my seat, looked over at her, and exhaled. "Damn, ma. I'm sorry. But, you already know I'm about to ride for you like I'm supposed to. Fuck Buddy. I gotta put you at the forefront of everything right now. Get you to safety while I handle my bidness. But first I got something for you."

Fifteen minutes later, I pulled on to the Mercedes Benz lot. By this time, Bree's face was cleansed and all she was doing was sniffling every now and then. "Yo, I know you thought I was going to forget about your birthday today, but nah, goddess. I could never do that." I rolled the car until I pulled up on the short, Jewish, Mercedes Benz dealer.

He stood in the empty parking space next to the one I pulled into with a smile on his face, and the sides of his curly hair blowing in the wind, because there was none on top of his head. His name was Gus, and Jeffery Grant had put me in with him, since the destruction of Brooklyn and

Harlem had been underway. "Baby, why are we here? Are you about to do what I think you are?" she asked, wiping her nose on a Kleenex.

I stepped out of the truck and shook hands with the white man. "Yo, I got the birthday girl sitting right there. Is her car ready?" I looked back at her. She had one hand covering her mouth as if she were in shock. Gus nodded, and waved for me to follow him.

"Sir, it's been ready since Thursday. The only reason I didn't allow for you to come and pick it up then, is because I wanted to inspect it myself. I was told to treat you with the utmost respect. So, if you'll follow me, I can take you to it."

Ten minutes later, I pulled the all-pink 2020 Mercedes Benz hard drop in front of Bree. It had all-white leather seats, four televisions. Her name was stitched in the head-rests, and there was a brand-new iPhone XS on the passenger's seat for her. I stepped out and handed her the keys. "Huh, ma, this is yours. I know it ain't much, but it's a peek at what's to come."

The sun reflected off of the new whip as she walked around the car in disbelief, running her finger along the paint as she traveled around it. Then, she sat in the driver's seat and lowered the top. Rubbed all over the leather seats, then looked into the ones behind her. "I don't know what to say. Kaleb, you're too much." She rushed out of the car and hugged me. Crashing into me with so much impact, we fell back against my truck.

"Yo, you deserve this and so much more, goddess. I got you from here on out, you hear me?" She nodded and hugged me tighter.

* * *

That night, I treated her to a nice romantic night out on the town. I kept telling her how beautiful she was to me. Not only because I knew it would make her feel good. But because it was the truth. Bree was a bad ass woman, and I wanted to cater to her and get her to see what I saw. We were both bigger than the projects we were raised in.

She was fairly quiet the entire night, but I noticed she stayed close on my arm as if she didn't want to let me go. When we left the restaurant and made it back to my truck, she took a deep breath, and turned to me. "Kaleb, are you gon' wind up kicking me to the curb, and getting with a woman that looks better than me. The reason I asked is because I saw how you were peeping Trinity. I mean, you wouldn't be wrong. I'm just, I don't know, a little worried because I'm falling for you pretty fast and I don't feel I'm worthy of such a man."

I was twenty years old. I didn't know how to honestly answer this question because I cared about her a lot, but at the same time, I was addicted to bad women and pussy. Bree was bad, and had a nice shot on her. I couldn't see myself kicking her to the curb for no other woman, but at the same time, I didn't want to paint myself in a corner and make it seem like I was done fucking with other females, because I wasn't.

The first thought that went through my head when I saw Trinity was that I wanted to know what she looked like bent over with me fucking her from the back. Every woman looked different getting hit from the back and she was so thick, I wanted to know. "Bree, I'll never kick you to the curb, ma. I care about you just as much as you care about me. On top of that, you're pregnant with my kid. What type of man would I be?"

"But, so is Rayven, and you're out with me tonight and not her. I mean, she has it all beauty, brains, money. I still can't understand how you've been spending so much time with me and not her. I'm a nobody. I can't offer you any-thing, but maybe a death sentence. So how long before I'm just an afterthought?"

I ain't gone even lie, I felt blindsided by that question. And, on top of that question, I felt like she was noncha-lantly trying to say I was shitting on Rayven, my other baby mother. That made me feel sick on the stomach, because it had been a minute since I'd checked in with her. Mostly because she had me blocked all over the place. But, I didn't think that was a good enough excuse. I should have been trying harder. "Yo, I'm bogus for not trying harder with Rayven. I ain't got no excuse for that. I will do better. For some reason, when it comes to you though, I feel like I just have to protect you and get you right, before I can allow you to be free in the slightest. Rayven ain't wanting or needing for nothing right now. She got me blocked all over the place. I don't know what's going to become of us. But right now, I just want to be here for you. I'll never kick you to the curb." I was sure of that.

"So, are we together then?" she asked and grabbed my hand.

"Bree, let's not complicate things. We still gotta figure out your housing, your money flow, your protection, and if we're going to have this baby. Us becoming an item is at the bottom of the totem pole. I'm just trying to get you through tomorrow. Buddy's hitta will be looking for you, that I know for sure." He'd called my phone again, con-firming the hit on Bree. He was dead serious, and I was worried.

She nodded. "Okay, Kaleb, but let me just ask you one last question, and I want the truth in one word. Okay?"

I nodded. "Come on wit it."

"Do you *really* love me?" She took a deep breath and looked into my eyes. I sat there for a minute thinking things over, and considered what we were up against on her behalf, and I knew without a shadow of a doubt that I was willing to ride with her.

"I do love you. No matter what we up against. I gotchu."

"Then that's enough for me." She pulled my head towards hers and planted a soft kiss on my lips.

## Chapter 8

"Yo, this heroin got me fucked up, son. I ain't been this numb in a long time. Word up," Pappy said, snorting a long line of the China White I had set out for him.

He was dark-skinned with long dreads, and a white eye he was blind in. He had a red rag around his neck, and I was able to make out the handles of both Glocks on his waist. Buddy had sent him to do Bree in, and the more I sat looking across the table at the young nigga, the more I wanted to fuck him over. He couldn't have been older than twenty. We sat at the table in my trap out in Brooklyn. We were waiting on Buddy to call so he could confirm the move was about to go down. Bree was already in the other room, anticipating what was to go down. Pappy didn't know she was already hip to the move scheduled. I wanted to break her into the game the right way.

He picked his head up from the table and pinched his nose. "Yo, I fuck wit Buddy the long way, kid. Ya Blood got all my lil niggas eating over in the Bronx. I'm talking lil kats like me that was starving before kid touched down from Harlem. Word up. He wanted to pay me twenty flat for this caper, but all I took was fifteen. I know he'll get me right in the long run. Besides, that bitch bogus. I'ma slice her ass up with these." He opened his Army fatigue jacket and showed me the handles of his two hunting knives. They had compasses on the ends of them. "Yeah these bitches a cut through bone, if you do it the right way."

He took the bottle of Seagram's gin, and turned it up. I sat across and watched his Adam's apple move up and down as he drank. My lip curling more and more as I imagined this bitch-ass nigga hurting Bree. "Yo, how old is you, Blood?"

### T.J. Edwards

"Nah, son, I ain't a Blood. I'm a Latin King from the Bronx, let's get that straight right away. And, to answer your question, I'm twenty as of last month. Why?" I shook my head.

"Just making casual conversation until Buddy call, that's it." I took a sip from the Moet I had on the table. "What got you into killing for that paper?" I asked.

"I kilt my first nigga when I was ten. Got into a fight wit him at school. Saw him the next day getting off of his bus, walked up to him and smoked his bitch ass. The old heads in the hood caught wind of what I did, and long story short, in a matter of weeks I was murdering for hire. They'd give me a gee a hit. Once I got older, I got smarter. Now, I ain't hitting a nigga up unless I'm getting fifteen stacks or better. If it's a bitch, I'll take ten. I hate hoez." He leaned his head down and tooted another line hard, then turned up the bottle of liquor. "What about you? How old were you when you smoked yo first nigga?"

I shrugged my shoulders. "I don't know, about thirteen or fourteen. Got tired of the nigga and his crew fucking wit me and Buddy, so I did what I had to. No biggie. Life goes on, and so do we. Nah mean?" I looked across the table at him. I could already envision the blood coming out random wounds in his body. This bitch-ass nigga had come into my trap, thinking he was about to hurt somebody I cared about like it was sweet. What he didn't know was that Buddy had set him up to meet the Reaper. I wasn't about to let nobody hurt Bree, or Breeyonna. Not while I was alive and able.

"You was a late bloomer, I see. By the time I was thirteen, I had fifteen niggas under my belt. I love killing shit. I even drive past the funeral homes of the people I smoked. It's a hell of a feeling." He smirked and pulled on his nose.

Bree came from the back of the house with an orange juice in her hand. "Kaleb, can I talk to you for a minute?" she asked, looking from me to him, then back to me again.

## Rise to Power 2

I scooted my chair backward. "Yo, I'll be back in a second, god. Let me see what's good wit her."

He rolled his eyes. "I can't wait for Buddy to call, son. I'm ready to get this over wit."

I followed Bree to the back room and closed the door. "What's good?"

"Kaleb, I'm freaking out. I don't know if I can go through wit this. I ain't never killed nobody before, and I'm scared to kill him. Word." She sat on the edge of the bed and looked up at me through wide brown eyes.

I knelt in front of her with a mug on my face. "Yo, fuck that nigga in there, Bree. That pussy represent Buddy and how Buddy really feels about you. This nigga here because he thinks I'm about to let him kill you, and you're telling me you're afraid to dead his bitch ass? Really?" I didn't understand.

The man in me couldn't grasp the fact that she was a female, and killing didn't come natural to most women like it did us men. I got angry because she was feeling how she was. Wanted to slap some sense into her. "I get all of that, Kaleb, but this is still murder. What if we get caught? Then what? Who's going to take care of Breeyonna, or our child that is on the way? Would you want me to give birth to your kid behind bars?"

"Yo, we ain't gon' get caught. We gon' pop that murder cherry that you got, and I'ma show you what's gon' happen to any nigga that try and come at you bogus. Word up. You carrying my seed now, ma. It's time you see how I really get down when it comes to me protecting mines." I stood up. "Now, stick to the script." I left out of the room, and almost bumped into Pappy.

He was standing outside of the door with his phone to his ear. He held up one finger, and pointed at it, covering the mouthpiece. "Yo, this Buddy on the phone right here. He just gave me the go-ahead and want to confirm it wit you. Huh." As he handed me the phone with his left hand, he pulled out one of the hunting knives with his right, and acted like he was about to go into my bedroom where Bree was.

I blocked his path. "Hold ya horses, kid. Let me get confirmation from Buddy so I can..." *Bam*! I swung the phone with all of my might and crushed it into his good eye, then punched him in the left temple as hard as I could. He dropped the knife and flew into the wall.

"Arrgh! Arrgh! My eye! My eye!" he hollered as blood ran down his cheek.

Bree swung open the door and covered her mouth. "Oh, my God."

I grabbed Pappy up, lifted him into the air and slammed him on his head, knocking him out cold. There was a big gash in his head leaking blood. His eyes were closed tight. He smelled as if he'd shit himself. "Yo, meet me in the other room. Now!" I ordered Bree, my chest heaving up and down. She nodded and rushed out of the hallway, into the other bedroom like I commanded of her.

I scooped up Pappy and carried him into the other room. Sat him in the chair and watched while Bree duct taped his ankles to the chair, and then his wrists. She slapped a piece of tape across his lips as well. Then stood back and looked up at me in a frenzy. "Now what, Kaleb?"

"Now you witness this G-shit firsthand, and I show you how you kill a rodent." I took the knife and slammed it into Pappy's thigh, and twisted the blade counter clockwise. His wound filled with blood and spilled over. His eyes opened with a start. He hollered into the duct tape, and slammed his back against the chair over and over. Sweat appeared on his brow. It dripped down the side of his face. He breathed heavily out of his nostrils. I twisted the knife some more, causing him to holler louder. Then I pulled it out of him and pointed the bloody blade into his face.

84

# Rise to Power 2

"You bitch-ass nigga. How dare you think you about to come into my trap, and kill the mother of my child? I don't know what that fuck nigga Buddy thought this was, but this ain't that, home boy." I smacked him with an open palm. His neck snapped to the right harshly. He struggled against his binds, breathing erratically. Groaning as if he was trying to tell me something, but I was in no mood to talk. Only kill. I wanted to see Bree kill his ass. I yearned to. "Come here, baby."

I reached out for Bree until she came alongside of me. I placed her body in front of mine, and placed the knife in her hand.

"I'm about to use this?" she asked through a cracking voice. I could feel her shaking like crazy. "Please don't make me do this, Kaleb. I'm so scared. I don't want him haunting me for the rest of my life. Please." She backed into me and tried to look up at me.

I got frustrated. "Kill this nigga, Bree. Slam this fucking blade in his neck, and I'll do the rest. Come on." I tried to maneuver the knife in her hand, but she wasn't going for it. She opened the fingers on her right hand and the knife fell to the carpet. I moved her out of the way and picked it up. Mugged her.

She backed away from me, and shook her head. "I'm sorry, Kaleb. I'm just not ready for that yet." I felt like spanking her ass until she cried. I was irritated. How was it she couldn't get the fact that you had to kill those that intended on killing you? It was how the game went. There was no way we could leave Pappy alive. He had to die. And, I was going to make her watch me.

"Aiight then, ma. But, you bet not look away, because not only was this nigga plannin' on killing you, but he was going to murder our unborn child as well. And, I don't know about you, but I don't let shit like that pass." I took the knife and slammed it into Pappy's jaw, and ripped it downward, leaving a big hole in it. He flopped around in the chair, still bound.

Blood poured out of his face and it excited me. He was screaming behind the tape, though it was muffled. Bree threatened to cover her face. I reached and pulled her hands away. "Nall, baby, watch this shit. This nigga Buddy about to have killas coming at us every single day. You gon' get used to me finishing niggas like this." I turned around and got to stabbing Pappy all over his face, over and over again. I went nuts. Slicing and jugging. Blood popped into the air and I kept on going. Furious that this nigga thought it was sweet. That he could come and do anything to Bree.

While I was murdering him, Bree stood behind me breathing hard. Every time the knife slammed into a certain part of his flesh, she would yelp, then attempt to cover her face and I would grab her hands away. Making her see what was to happen to any of our enemies that were sure to come because of Buddy, and the dread heads. A part of me snapped. I couldn't control myself and Pappy wound up sitting in the chair, receiving stab after stab until his face was unrecognizable.

He fell forward onto the carpet, in a puddle of his own mess. I stood with the knife in my hand, dripping onto the carpet. Bree was squatting in the corner of the room with her arms around her knees. Tears dripped down her pretty face. I dropped the knife on top of Pappy's chest. It bounced off and fell to the carpet. Made my way to Bree, and sat beside her.

"Baby, are you okay?" I asked and pulled up her head so I could see her face.

"That's my first time seeing somebody get killed like that. It's freaking me out. I think I'm going to be sick." She covered her mouth with one hand and dry heaved. "I'm sorry, Kaleb, all this is new to me. I'll get better if I have to, but this is just—wow."

# Rise to Power 2

I looked over at Pappy's dead body. There was blood coming out of his face steadily. His mouth was wide open. He laid on his left cheek. There was a puddle formed around his head. I took a deep breath, and shrugged my shoulders. "Fuck that nigga. It had to happen. This punk thought he was about to come in here and kill you like I wasn't gon' do shit. That nigga Buddy thinking he calling shots like that now? Really?"

I jumped up, and kicked Pappy as hard as I could in his ribs, flipping his ass on to his back. "Man, fuck these niggas. Like I said before, I got you now. And this is what it is. Get up." I grabbed her hand and pulled her to her feet.

She stood up and looked at me for a short period, before wrappin' her arms around my body. "I'm sorry I'm reacting this way, Kaleb. I know you did this for me, and I love you for it. I'll get better, you'll see." She stepped on her tippy toes and kissed my lips hard. Slid her tongue into my mouth and moaned.

I could have sworn while she was kissing me that I saw Pappy's soul slowly sit up from his body, then turn around to look at me mugging, before it shook its head and walked through the wall of the room, disappearing. I didn't feel one way or the other. It wasn't the first time I had seen a person I'd killed. I'd been seeing the victims do that ever since I was a teenager.

I tongued Bree down and rubbed all over her ass. "Yo, it's time I put you up somewhere safe so I can go at this nigga's people, head on."

She shook her head. "Nall, I'm coming wit you. I don't want something happening to you and then I'm not there to hold you down like I'm supposed to. That would break my heart in half." I didn't know what to say to her, because I already had my mind made up. So, I simply held her close and rested my lips against her cheek.

T.J. Edwards

## Chapter 9

Instead of Buddy getting out when he was supposed to, the police in Newark, New Jersey, wound up putting a hold on him for the cities of Brooklyn and Philadelphia. They said he had outstanding warrants in both places. And, even though his bail had been paid for the infraction with their city, they were forced to keep him in custody. It was a blow for him, and a chance for me to get Bree, Breeyonna and myself together before his feet were able to hit the pavement. So, after the bail bondsman gave me this information, I paid him, and started to get things in order.

I copped Bree and Breeyonna a nice, three-bedroom house out in Yonkers, New York, right off of Bush Avenue. It was a quiet area dominated by older, retired white folks. There was a police patrol car that cruised through the area every fifteen minutes. There was also two other deputies on bike patrol that took the liberty of knocking on the residents' doors, checking in on them to make sure they were safe and sound. I liked that part. Even though I didn't fuck with the law like that, I still needed to know that when I wasn't around physically to protect Bree and Breeyonna, they would be safe and sound.

I had so many things going on inside of my brain that I needed to take comfort in the fact that they were okay. The third day after she'd moved in, I gave Bree my Visa and allowed her to go crazy, purchasing everything she needed for the house, in order to make it feel like home for her and Breeyonna. She took the card, and headed off with Breeyonna in her Benz, while Rayven hit me up, saying that it was urgent that we have a sit-down.

An hour later, I sat across from her in her living room, wondering what was going on. She took two wine glasses out of the kitchen. Sat them on the table in front of us, and filled them halfway with the red liquid. She was dressed in a pair of Prada jeans, and the matching top, her belly poking out of it. Her long hair fell down her back. Curly. Now it was past her waist. I was guessing the pregnancy was physically doing her justice.

She looked good. She took one of the glasses and sat it in front of me. Then smiled. "Why are you looking so angry?"

I pushed the glass away. "What's good wit you, man? You made it sound on the phone like it was real urgent and shit."

She sat down across from me and crossed her legs. Took a sip of the wine, and sat the glass back on the table. Her condo was laid out. I was wondering why we were meeting here and not at our place in Queens. "First off, I've missed your evil ass. Secondly, I've acquired two more restaurants for you. A Sonic and a Wendy's. They weren't cheap, but the return on both of them will be worth it down the line." She took the paperwork out of her Gucci bag, and slid it across the table to me.

I saw right away that the properties were in my name. I was confused. "Why are you looking out for me? I thought we were on bad terms. I ain't been here in over three weeks. You got me blocked all over the place. What gives?" I sat the papers down and looked across the table at her, reading her body language as best I could.

She lowered her head, and took a deep breath. "Kaleb, I miss you. I don't know what you're doing over there with Bree, if that's where you are, but I ain't backing out without a fight. You and I have been through too much together." She pulled up her shirt. "Does this ring a bell?" She rubbed all over her stomach.

The belly button looked darker and it stood out just a pinch. The sight of it made me feel some type of way. I got up and sat on the couch beside her. Placed my hand on her stomach and rubbed all over it. Dropped to my knees and kissed it.

"Yo, I don't know what you want from me, Rayven. You already know I still love you. I think about you every single day. Wondering when we're going to get this shit right. You've always been special to me. You know that." I laid my cheek on her belly and kissed it. Rubbing in a circle.

She rubbed my cheek. "Kaleb, do you love her?" She took my chin and tilted my head upward. Looked me in the eyes. "I want you to be truthful."

I slid back on the couch beside her and placed my hand on her stomach. "I care about her. I don't want to see nothing bad happen to her, or Breeyonna. If I can protect them from any harm, then I am." I met her eyes and saw hurt in them.

She pushed my hand away and stood up. I could tell the task of standing and sitting with such a big belly was becoming harder and harder for her to do. She stood, then started to pace. "I don't get it. She ain't got nothin'. What could you possibly see in her? Me and you have come from the gutter together. Not to mention, it's been you and I that have seen to it that your mother landed in the right hands to get the best possible care. Bree ain't have nothing to do wit it. I am confused right now." Her eyes began to water. She blinked and tears came out of them. She wiped them away and began mumbling.

I stood up and blocked her path. Grabbed both of her arms and held her. She refused to make eye contact with me. "Rayven, just because I care about her, don't mean that I don't love you. Damn, we ain't gotta be divided like this. You've always been my heart. You know that."

She jerked away from me and backed all the way up. "How! How, Kaleb? How am I your heart, when you haven't been over here to check on me in weeks. And, don't give me that shit about me having you blocked, because if you really cared about me, you would have tracked me down and found me. We live together in Queens. You know about my condo here in Manhattan, so what is your excuse? What is your excuse for leaving your side of the bed cold every night? For leaving me to fend for myself while I'm pregnant with our first child? Huh? When meanwhile, you're over there fucking a bitch that already has a child, and a baby father. It's not fair. You are losing your fucking mind, and making me lose mine as well. I expect so much better from you." She turned her back, and hugged her self.

I stood there in silence. My brain spinning like crazy. Bree crossed my mind, she had yet to send me a text, letting me know she had made it home safely from furniture and house shopping. I had to shake my head to get out of her zone. Came back to reality, and thought about what Rayven was saying. "Rayven, I'm sorry, baby. I didn't mean for you to feel as if I am putting anybody before you, because that's not the case. I mean, I have been if we look at it how you just said it, but I swear I didn't mean to. Shorty just in a fucked-up position right now. That nigga Buddy tried to have one of his lil homie's kill her the other day. Had I not been there, she would have been a goner."

Rayven shrugged her shoulders. "To be honest with you, I don't care about Bree. Fuck her. I wish that nigga would have laid her flat out. It would make things a lot easier for us." She scoffed and took a seat on the couch. "I just never thought that we would be here. Not Kaleb and Rayven. The two project kids that swore they would make it out of the slums. That we would be something great. We vowed to have each other's backs through it all. We vowed to never allow anybody to penetrate our bond. I really can't believe that it is Bree's bum ass that's doing it. A bitch that already has a kid. Really? She can't benefit you in no way. I just don't get it." She took a sip of her wine.

"Rayven, are you even supposed to be drinking that shit like that with my baby inside of you?" I came over and picked the glass up from the table. She shrugged her shoulders. "It's better than me smoking a blunt right now. Or tooting a line of cocaine. That's what I really want to do. I ain't never did that shit before in my life, but I would love to do it right now." She exhaled loudly.

I felt like snapping and cursing her ass out. But instead, I held my temper. Kept my comments to myself. I felt like I'd taken her through a lot. That it was my turn to bend just a little bit for her. I needed to try and restore the bit of love that she still had for me. I sat the glass back on the table and knelt in front of her. Kissed her knee.

"Baby, what can I do for you? Just name it, and it's done." I kissed her inner thigh and bit it through her jeans. She pushed me away.

"Get away from me, Kaleb. I ain't feeling you in that light no more. I don't know where your lips have been." She frowned and mugged me with her pretty eyes. I moved her hands out of the way, and started to kiss up and down her inner thighs. Placed my nose right where her kitty lips were pressing against the material. Sniffed hard, then licked the denim.

"Damn, ma." I started to unbutton her jeans.

She tried to fight me off. "Nall, gon', Kaleb. I'm serious. I hate you right now. I hate your guts. How could you ever choose that bitch over me? We've been through so much. You and I."

I pulled her jeans to the bottom of her calf muscles. Then slid her panties to the side, sniffing her hole. Licked the lips, and sucked on them, before popping them out of my mouth. They were bald and golden. Hot and smelled like strawberries. I opened them with my thumbs, and licked all around her clitoris that was protruded out. Pulled her pants all the way off of her ankles, and threw them across the room.

She placed both of her feet on the couch, bussing her pussy wide open for me to do my thing. I sniffed all over it, then started to tongue fuck her while she held my head. "Uh! No! No! Get away from me, Kaleb. I hate you! I hate you!" She forced my face further into her gap, rising from the couch and riding my face as she got wetter and wetter.

Her pregnant belly bumped into my forehead. Pulled my eyebrows backwards, but it didn't stop me from attacking that pussy. Getting nasty with her. Her thick thighs were spread wide. "I'm sorry, ma. I'm sorry." I licked up and down her slit. Rubbed my face in it. She reached between her legs and pinched her clit, just like she used to when we were twelve and she was afraid to let me fuck. "When are you going to forgive daddy? Huh? When you gon' forgive me?" I sucked her clit into my mouth, and ran my tongue from side to side. She was so wet that it ran down the side of my cheek. I slid two fingers inside of her, and went to town at full speed, while sucking on her clit.

She screamed. "Daddy! Daddy! I swear to God, I hate you! Uhf! Uhf! Shit!" She wrapped her red thighs around her head and came all over my face, humping into it. Screaming louder and louder. It was so much juice that I was being smothered. I couldn't breathe to save my life. Until finally, she opened her legs, exposing her gash. It was glistening with juices. The golden lips looked wrinkled, and oh so good to me.

Rabbit came and sat on the floor a short distance from us. Lifted her short skirt, and ran her fingers through her pink, bald, pussy. "You guys are so hot. I watched you eat her out, and it's so hot. Geez, I'm serious." She undid the straps on her blouse to expose her breasts. They were nice and round. Perky, with big pink nipples that stood erect.

# Rise to Power 2

Rayven slid to the edge of the couch, then straddled me, after pushing me backward. "I'm finna ride this dick, Kaleb, but it don't mean nothing. I swear it don't mean nothing." She undid my pants, slid them down to my ankles, my boxers along with them.

My dick sprang up like a broomstick handle. She licked all over it before sliding me into her mouth, holding it with two hands. Sucking fast and hard with her big booty in the air. Juices oozing out of her pussy hole. Rabbit crawled over and stuck her face between Rayven's legs from the back. Spread her ass cheeks, and began darting her tongue in and out of her asshole. Rayven perked up, and looked behind her. Moaned and closed her eyes, then started to suck me faster, gagging.

Rabbit's titties wobbled and shook while she took advantage of Rayven. I was trying to watch my dick go in and out of Rayven's mouth, and Rabbit's titties at the same time. I wanted to see her pussy again. It looked so fresh and ripe. I wondered what it felt like. I had never fucked a white bitch before and looking at her body, she had me wondering what it would be like to test that ass out. Word up. I could feel Rayven's juices dripping onto my thighs. She reached under herself, held me steady, then slid down my pole. Holding my shoulders, she sank down and started to ride me nice and slow at first. I pulled her shirt up so her breasts were bared. They were fuller, equipped with milk. I held them in my hands and squeezed them, making her throw her head back and moan out loud.

"Fuck! Daddy, you're playing wit my titties. They got milk in them. Uh! Fuck! They got milk in them." Rabbit turned her back to me and bent over. Stuck her face between our sexing parts. I could feel her tongue licking at my dick, while Rayven rode me. She sucked one of my balls into her mouth. Moaned out loud, then slid her fingers back into her crease. I could see everything from my vantage point. It looked so fucking good. Her lil pink pussy was oozing. I grabbed her by the hip and pulled her to me. She looked over her shoulder and licked her lips. Spread her knees, and popped her ass out at me. I could see her essence all over her thick pussy lips.

"Touch me, Kaleb. Touch my white pussy. It's okay. I need you to." She backed up closer to me, and sucked Rayven's right nipple into her mouth. Rayven moaned and threw her head back. Riding me faster and faster, with her hands on my chest. "I'm riding my daddy. I'm riding my daddy. Oh! I missed this. I missed this, daddy. Fuck."

She grabbed a handful of Rabbit's hair, and they began to make out all loud and nasty, while she hopped up and down on my dick. I used the distraction to slide my hand into Rabbit's crease from the back. Played over her bald lips. Smushed them together, before sliding my middle finger up her hole. She shrieked and spread her knees further apart again. It looked like she was trying to do the splits. Her pussy felt hot, and real tight. Almost as if she hadn't ever been fucked, but I knew better. I didn't understand, but now I was feening to see what that hole was like.

Rayven bounced up and down. "Kaleb. Kaleb! I'm cumming, daddy! I'm cumming. Oh my God, I'm cumming!" She screamed and started to bounce higher and higher, digging her nails into my chest, before splashing all over me. She hopped off of my dick, and sat her pussy right on my lips, riding me some more. My tongue shot out of my mouth, searching for her button, licking and swallowing her juices. Her moans got louder and louder.

Rabbit crawled around. Took my dick in her little fist, and pumped it up and down five times, before sucking me into her mouth. Taking me to the back of her throat, pulling me out, then doing it again. She rubbed my black dick all over her white face and sniffed it.

## Rise to Power 2

"Damn, this is a lot of meat. You're strapped, Kaleb. I don't think you'd fit in me." She stood up and rubbed the big head of my pipe in between her pink pussy lips, getting off on the feel of it, and teasing me in the process. Her pussy felt like a velvet furnace. "I got shivers all over my body while I ate Rayven's cat. Un! Un! This big black dick! Fuck! I wanna put it in me so bad! Please, can I, Rayven? Just once! Just once!"

My head went in and out of her lips faster and faster. She looked like a little white girl playing with a grown black man's dick. Rayven popped her hips, turned around on my face so her back was facing me, and opened her pussy lips wider to feel my tongue. "Bitch, no! No! This is my daddy. My daddy. Un! He only fucks his baby. Un! Shit! I'm cumming, daddy! I'm cumming!" She threw her head back and screamed.

She fell off of me, and landed on her back with her legs wide open. Rabbit rushed and stuck her face between her legs, licking up and down her slit, opening them wide and slurping from her hole hungrily. The noises she made had my dick jumping up and down. Then, the sight of her ass in the air, with the bald pink pussy that poked out of the cheeks were driving me mad. I got up and knelt behind her. Running my dick up and down her crease. The lips opened and more juices poured out of her. She arched her back and groaned. I rubbed all over that ass, wanting to fuck her so bad, just to see what that white shit was like.

My niggas from Harlem was always talking about they were snowed-in, meaning they were white girl crazy, and I never understood why, until I saw Rabbit's pink gash bussed open the way that it was. I ran the head in between her lips, and sawed it up and down her slit. My head felt so sensitive that I was seconds away from cumming already.

"Please let him fuck me, Rayven. I'll do anything. Anything. Please. I need that black dick in me, now." She rocked backward and her pussy sucked in about two inches of my dick. Searing the head. My eyes rolled backward. I took a deep breath, and held her steady.

As much as I wanted to fuck, I couldn't disrespect Rayven like that. There had to be a reason she didn't want me to fuck this white bitch. "No! That's my daddy." She rushed to me, and straddled my lap again. Riding me as fast as she could. I laid back and held her hips. Closed my eyes, and imagined I was fucking Rabbit, only for a moment, then opened them, and enjoyed Rayven popping that ass in my lap.

Her pussy was even wetter than before. It felt so good, that I had to dig my nails into her ass meat. Rabbit came over and straddled my face, started to make out with Rayven. I opened my eyes, and saw how pretty her pink pussy looked. Swiped at it with my tongue. Tasting her. She tasted different, unlike Rayven, or Bree. Even her scent was different. I sucked on her left pussy lip, and then the right. Slid my tongue into her as far as it could go. She opened her lips wide and moaned.

Above me, her and Rayven were licking all over each other. Rabbit squeezed Rayven's breasts until milk eased out of her nipples and ran down her stomach, on to her hips. This made Rayven ride me faster and faster. I couldn't take it anymore. The next thing I knew, I was cumming back to back in my baby mother's tight womb. Nutting. She felt it and tensed up, threw her head back again, and came all over me in spasms. Rabbit ground her pelvis into my face and came against my flickering tongue. "Uh! Kaleb, one day I'ma ride this black dick," she screamed.

## Chapter 10

"Like I said, son, we haven't heard from Destiny ever since she left this morning for school. The principal said he saw her walk into the building this morning, but her home room teacher said that she's been absent the entire day. I'm so worried, I'm losing my mind," my mother said, getting out of her bed, and pacing the floor.

It had been three months since she'd arrived at the new hospital. Not only did she have a short curly afro now, but she'd gained about ten pounds, and she looked healthier. She shook her head, then turned to Derez. "It is your job, Derez, to keep an eye on your sister. Yours. How dare you leave her side, just so you can flirt with a bunch of tramps. I feel like kicking your ass. I swear," she said with her face balled up.

He lowered his head, and took a deep breath. "It's not my fault, Mama, me and Destiny always split up once we get onto the playground. She go her way and I go mine. It's not fair for you to blame this on me. Maybe she's off messing with one of her boyfriends." He picked a piece of lint off of his pants and flicked it. Picked up his phone and dialed a number. My mother balled up her fist and looked as if she was ready to rush across the room at him.

Rayven stepped into her way and hugged her. "It's okay, Mama, we're going to find her. You don't need to stress yourself out. We're on it." She kissed her lips, and hugged her for a long time.

My mother closed her eyes, as tears began to seep out of them. I sat on the couch, not knowing what to do, or what to think. It was so unlike Destiny to just go missing. I was worried out of my mind but I knew that I had to put on a brave face for everybody else. Had I worn my heart on my sleeve in this moment I was sure that everybody would have had an emotional breakdown, and that would have crushed me even more, so I played cool, even though my mind was racing.

I got up, and took my mother into my arms. Kissed her forehead. "It's good, queen. We gon' give Destiny a few more hours to turn up, if she don't, then your son is going to into action. All you gotta do is remain calm. Let me do my thing. You hear me?" I kissed her soft cheek and held her tighter. She melted in my arms, looking up at me. I glanced out of the windshield and saw about ten Crip niggas, with blue rags hanging out of their left pockets, mugging my truck. I could tell they were ready to get on bullshit because we had been parked there for a minute. I wanted to lace my brother wit a little bit of game, but right then was not the right time.

One of the Crip niggas pulled out a handgun and aimed it at my truck. Then pointed it in the air and bussed twice as a warning. I nodded in understanding and rolled past the stop sign, out of their hood. Got on the expressway. "Yo, Derez, I don't want you to idolize me. Every day, I run the risk of getting killed. All of that money you saw is dirty. Niggas had to lose their lives for it, one way or the other. The way I'm living, I'm on borrowed time. This shit can't last that much longer. Sooner or later, my time is going to run out. But, by that time, I just want to make sure that you, Moms and Destiny are all well taken care of. I'm sacrificing myself so that y'all ain't never gotta get out here in these streets. So, hearing you talking like that is a gut punch to me. It's bananas, kid. You feel me?"

Derez nodded. "I do, but we ain't never had no father, Kaleb. It's always been you taking care of us, even when Mama was healthy. I knew who it was that was buying all of my Jordans and Timbs. Destiny knew who paid for her to get braces on her teeth, and all of her nice clothes, jewelry, make up and accessories. I mean, we know Mama tried to do the best she could, but it was hard on her. You stepped up to the plate, so why wouldn't I want to idolize you for that alone?" He looked out of his window, and took a deep breath. Shook his head, then grabbed the apple juice from the console, sipping from it. and shook her head.

That night, I rolled out to the Red Hook Houses in Brooklyn, dropped off fifty kilos of heroin and two kilos of pure Hong Kong Fentanyl. I picked up seven hundred and fifty thousand, before rolling out, with my sister on my mind like crazy. It was eleven at night and still there had been no word from Destiny, and I was feeling sick on the stomach.

Derez sat in my passenger's seat with a mug on his face. He took a blunt out of his shirt pocket and licked it up and down. "I'm starting to panic. Yo, I'm missing my sister, man. Word up." He sparked the blunt, and took three strong pulls from it, and blew the smoke toward the ceiling of the roof, coughing.

I continued to roll through Brooklyn. There were people out everywhere. All in the middle of the street. Grouped up on the sidewalk in front of the many brownstones. Little kids were jumping rope as if it were normal to be out so late. "Yo, when you start blowing, kid?" I asked, feeling some type of way.

He held the smoke in for as long as he could. He made a clicking sound the longer he held it. Then, he blew it to the ceiling. "Yo, I been blowing since I was eleven. I thought you knew. Destiny smoke too, but not as much as me." He laughed, and took another stronger pull. Tried to pass it to me.

I took it out of his hand and stubbed it out in my ashtray. "Bruh, this ain't cool. Moms know about it?" I asked, ready to buss him in his chest. I felt offended. He was only thirteen. In my book that was too young to be smoking. I didn't give a fuck what the streets of New York said. I didn't want my little brother or sister following in my footsteps. I wanted them to be better than me. Smoking was the gateway for him to become a savage. At least it's how I felt.

"Yeah, she know. You know Destiny talk too much. Mama smoke too, but I think it's more to ease her pain then anything. But, she do know. I don't know how she feel about it. She didn't say much. She was kind of sick at the time that she found out."

"Yeah, well, I don't like it. You don't need that bullshit. I want you and Destiny to have a better life than me and Rayven had. Y'all going to college so you can be somebody. That's my word."

Derez waved me off. "Nall, son, I ain't fucking wit school for that long. I'm trying to have chips like you, Dunn, word up." He wiped his nose, and sat back in his seat. Trying his best to look hard. This only infuriated me in the worst way. I waited until I pulled up to a stop sign right in front of the Bed Stuy Projects, and turned to him.

"Yo, my word, if you keep talking like that, I'ma buss ya ass. I don't give a fuck how cool you think being a thug is. It ain't happening for you, lil brother. You gon' make it out of New York and do great things with your life. It's more to the world than what you think you know. Trust me on that."

He looked out of his window, and acted as if he wasn't trying to hear what I was saying. "Son, you got mad chips. Yo, I know that bag you placed in the trunk was full of cash. All the niggas who older brothers hussle say you're out here doing ya thing. It's because of you that they respect me now. You're riding a Benz truck and everything. Rayven's pushing a BMW, and even Bree is rolling a Benz. I know it's all because of you. Why would I want to finish school when you didn't have to? Yo, I just wanna ball, but have band-os all over the city, and make other niggas do the leg work for me. I wanna have plenty bad bitches. Hoez that live to cater to me. Nah mean? Yo, let's roll out them Crip niggas mugging us hard," he said, looking out of his window.

His eyes were bucked. I had to keep rolling because I was stuck in that moment. I didn't know what to say to my little brother, because everything that he'd just said made sense. My father was a deadbeat nigga. A no-show. It was like he'd given up on my mother and all of us, and refused to show up. I didn't know if he was alive, or dead. But as crazy as it may sound, I still yearned for my old man. I wanted to know who he was. How he acted? How he looked? I just wanted to kick it with him for one day. I had so many questions for him, and a part of me loved him. I didn't know why, but I just did.

While growing up, I hated to see my mother struggling to make ends meet. Some nights, she didn't even know where our next meal would come from. When it came to the bills, she'd be up late into the wee hours of the night, crying her eyes out because she wasn't sure if we'd be kicked out of our project apartment by the end of that month. Our clothes were bummy. Hand-me-downs from churches, friends, and older relatives. I hated seeing all of that, so I jumped off the stoop early and got into the game. Robbing, stealing, and doing whatever I had to, to make it happen for her and my little brothers and sisters. My mother was my heart and soul. I felt that it was my job as a young man, and a grown man to do what I had to, to make sure that she was secure in all areas of life.

Never once did I stop to think that my little brother and sister were paying attention to everything I was doing. "Yo, Derez, I ain't have a choice coming up. I ain't have a big brother like me that gave a fuck like I do about you. I see a star inside of you, kid, something great. It's my job to make sure you become all that you were meant to be. These streets are made for inevitable losers. That's it. Niggas that were born to lose. You were born to win, and I'ma hold you down until you do. That's my word." I grabbed the back of his head and brought his cheek to my lips, kissing him like I always did.

He smiled. "Yeah, I guess you're right, Kaleb. Besides, I just wanted to be like you when I got older. Pushing Benzes and all that shit, nah mean? But, if you're saying the streets are for losers, then I gotta find another way."

* * *

That night, Rayven became overly emotional. More emotional than I had ever seen her before. Me and Derez got to our home out in Queens sometime after midnight. When I opened the door, Rayven was sitting in the living room, reading *King of New York: Blueprints of a Legend,* on her phone. She had the lights out, with candles burning. I flipped the light switch and saw that she was sitting there with tears in her eyes.

When she saw me, she jumped up and rushed over to me, hugging my neck. "Baby, please tell me you found her? None of us has been able to locate Destiny and she ain't hit nobody's phone. I'm so worried." She hugged me tight and started to break down.

I waved Derez off. He walked out of the room, and headed upstairs toward his bedroom. "Baby, calm down. I'm sure she's okay. I'm hoping she's over one of her friend's houses and just didn't want to be bothered. I mean, I know that's farfetched, but it's the only thing keeping my brain clear right now." I was getting sicker by the minute, but I couldn't admit that to her.

She was eight months pregnant. She didn't need the stress of seeing me lose myself. I had to be strong for everybody around me. I felt if I didn't, they'd all crumble, and then so would I. I was able to stay strong because I knew I had to. But, I was literally inches away from losing myself. Rayven took my hand and led me out of the living room, upstairs to our bedroom, where she made me take my shirt off and climb into the bed with her. Once there, she rubbed up and down my stomach muscles. Laid her head on my chest, and was quiet for a long time, before breaking her silence. "Baby, Buddy is out."

I sat all the way up. Her head fell off of me and onto the bed. "What? When did they let him out?" I asked, hopping out of the bed and throwing my shirt over my head. My heart was beating fast as hell. I pulled my phone from my pocket and got ready to call Bree.

"He got out yesterday at midnight. I just found out about this because he called me." She slid out of the bed, holding her stomach. "Baby, he needs to be out here taking care of his baby mother and daughter. Not you. I could give birth any day now. I need you by my side." She tried to hug me, but I stepped back.

"Wait a minute, why would Blood call you? What the fuck you got to do with him getting out?" I asked, looking at her very suspiciously. Something wasn't right. I could feel it deep within the pits of my soul.

Rayven turned her back on me and climbed back into the bed. "I don't feel like arguing wit you right now, Kaleb. I just want my man back. She's had enough of you. We're about to start a family. There is no need for her to be in the middle of us, when she has a whole ass baby daddy already. Damn, I'm sorry." She broke into tears.

I wasn't trying to hear that shit. "Yo, what the fuck did you do, Rayven? I ain't gon' ask you no more. Tell me!" I snapped.

Her crying intensified. She shook her head with her face covered. Tears seeped out of the cracks of her fingers. Ran down her wrist. "I ain't do shit! Damn, Kaleb! I did

T.J. Edwards

what I was supposed to do! I'm fighting for us. You're my man. Not that bitch's!" she hollered at the top of her lungs. Then, she grabbed her stomach and wailed in pain. Opened her legs and her water broke. "Oh my God!" She looked down, then reached out for me. I stood there for a minute too long, head spinning, not knowing what to do.

I had Bree on my mind heavy. I knew Buddy would go at her full steam ahead, before he came at me. I was sure he was still thinking murder, and that was if it hadn't already been done. Then, the thought of something serious happening to Destiny really spooked me. Buddy was evil, even more so than me. He was the type to attack all soft targets. Mothers, siblings and kids. He didn't care. He and Destiny had never gotten along. Ever since she was a little girl, she had always called him ugly and told him he stunk. I was sure he wouldn't have any problem killing her. Suddenly, I felt sick on my stomach. I rushed to Rayven's side and propped pillows behind her head. "Derez, come here, Dunn!"

Derez ran into the room in his pajamas, rubbing cold out of his eyes. "Yeah, what up?" he asked, yawning with his fist in front of his mouth. His eyes were bloodshot. "My baby mother about to have my seed right now. Come on, we gotta get her into my truck, and to the hospital. Now!"

106

# Chapter 11

Rayven held onto my shirt as I tried to pry her hands off of me. The doctors wanted to rush her into the emergency room. They said she was having our baby tonight and the child was already beginning to crown. I was in a panic. She was just a week past her eighth month. I didn't know what that meant for the health of our child, but I was thinking the worst.

On top of that, Bree had not answered any of my calls. That concerned me, because she never took more than a few seconds to return my texts or messages. I didn't know whether to stay at the hospital with Rayven, or to go out and find Bree. Not to mention, Destiny was still missing as well. My life seemed to be spiraling out of control. Going too fast for me to be able to keep us with.

"You gotta come in here with me, Kaleb. I'm so scared. I can't do this without you. I just can't. Please don't make me," she whimpered. Reaching out for my shirt again. It was all wrinkled and stretched because of her.

"Sir, you need to tell her something, because we have to get her prepped for delivery right now. The baby's head is crowning as we speak," the young, Jewish doctor reported.

My mind was racing. This was my firstborn. I needed to be here to see my kid being born, but at the same time, I had to find Bree and my sister. Their lives depended on me finding them as soon as possible. From what I heard, labor took hours and hours. I could be here for two days and that would spell death for Bree and Destiny.

"Please don't do this to me, Kaleb. Please don't make me have this baby on my own." Now she was crying. Snot came out of her nose. Her face was bright red. She reminded me of herself as a young girl. Back then, she was

very emotional and cried a lot. Everything hurt her feelings. Especially if I said anything that was meant for a joke,
but she'd taken it wrong.

I had the power of life or death in my tongue when it
came to her. I looked into her face and couldn't deny her
of my presence. It was my responsibility to be there. I had
to hold her down. "I got you, Rayven, let's do this."

Even though those were the words that came out of my
mouth, my mind was heavy with Bree and Destiny. I worried about Breeyonna just a bit, but I couldn't see Buddy
hurting his own daughter. The nurses rushed me into an
area of the hospital where they made me strip off my street
clothes and put on scrubs. After that, my arms were
scrubbed all the way to the elbow, and then my hands, in a
big sink. They placed latex gloves on my hands, and cov-
erings on my AirMax, and led me to the delivery room.

When I got in there, Rayven was laid on her back, huff-
ing and puffing. Her ankles had already been placed in stir-
rups. There was a doctor between her legs, and a nurse on
each side of him. I rushed to Rayven's side and took her
hand into mine. As soon as it made contact, she squeezed
it so hard I wanted to head butt her ass so that she released
it. The pain was serious.

She hollered and continued to pant. "Kaleb, I hate you
right now. I hate you. You did this shit to me. You put this
big-head-ass baby in me. You son of a bitch! Aw!" she hollered.

I rubbed her pretty face. Picked up the cloth a nurse had
given me and dabbed at the sweat on her forehead. "It's
good, baby. We gon' be alright. Just get our lil one out.
Please." She continued to pant. She closed her eyes, and
pushed as best she could. Her face was a dark red. The
edges along her hair lining were curled up. Her neck was
wet with sweat, before I cleaned it up.

# Rise to Power 2

I kissed her on the forehead and laid my cheek against hers. Below, the doctor was busy at work. The nurses looked on. "Okay, I'm going to need you to push as hard as you can, ma'am. We're almost at the finish line. Give me your best shot."

Rayven sat up on her elbows, panting. She frowned her face. Closed her eyes and pushed, straining. Her face now taking on the hue of purple. "Uh!" She breathed, then fell to her pillow with her chest heaving up and down.

"That was good. Take a mini rest, and I'm going to need you to try a little harder. We're almost there," the doctor assured her.

Rayven shook her head. "I can't do this. I can't. I don't have any more energy. This baby's head is too big. It's all your fault, Kaleb. Everybody in your family got big ass heads. I should have known," she cried, shaking her head from side to side.

I wanted to laugh, but I knew that wouldn't have went over well. Instead, I leaned into her face, and kissed her lips. Laid my face against her cheek again. "Do it for me, baby. Handle this bidness. Bring our lil one into the world, so we can be a family. I need you right now. We both do," I said, stroking her long pretty hair.

She rose to her elbows and pushed as hard as she could, while I hugged her to my chest and kissed her face. "Ahh! Get! Out! Of! Me!" Her fists were balled up, with the sheets inside of them. Her toes curled, and I heard her pass gas more than once.

After three hours of this, finally, I could hear our baby screaming at the top of its lungs. I looked down and saw the doctor pull it out, holding it a short distance away from her pussy, now open like a foxhole. The nurse wrapped somethin' around the umbilical cord and looked up to me. "Sir, do you want to cut the cord?" she asked.

## T.J. Edwards

I released Rayven's hand and took the scissors from her hand. The nurse guided me as I snipped the cord. It made me feel like a king. Especially when they cleaned my child off just enough to place her in my arms. She cried and kicked her little legs. Her gray eyes were opened wide, before she closed them. The hair on her head was wavy and silky. Her head shaped like those in my family, just like Rayven had said it would be.

I held her to my chest and broke into tears. She was so beautiful. I sat on the bed bedside Rayven and showed her to her. She moved her gown back and unwrapped our daughter. Allowed her to feel her skin on skin. It sent a chill through me. Before her birth, the whole pregnancy thing had seemed real to me, but not as real as holding my actual child in my arms. Somethin' about it made me emotional, and then angry. I would protect this baby and Rayven with my life. It was like seeing our daughter made me look at Rayven in a far different light. Instead of seeing a girl I had been in love with my entire life, now I was seeing my queen. The woman I would surely marry and do right by. I had to set an example for my daughter right away. Had to make her mother a wife, and not just a baby mother. It was crazy how that wisdom came to me in those few minutes after her birth.

Rayven handed her back to me and situated herself so that she was resting on my chest. "I'm so tired, Kaleb. Everything on me hurts. Everything." She closed her eyes, while the nurse stitched her up down below. "I just want you to love me from here on out. Let's be a team. Ex out the rest of the world if it isn't your mother or siblings." She breathed heavily, squeezing her eyes tighter.

I wrapped my arm around her, and held our daughter in my right arm. "What are we going to name her, baby?" I asked, looking over her features. She looked so exotic.

"I don't know, baby. Let's think about it for a few days, and go from there."

Sometime that night, my phone buzzed with a call from Bree. When I answered the phone, she sounded hysterical. "Kaleb! Buddy's out. He took Breeyonna and now he's trying to kill me. You gotta help me. Please. I've been shot," she screamed into the phone.

I could hear a heavy flow of cars in her background. Her breathing was heavy. It sounded like she was running. "What do you mean shot?" I asked, sitting up. "Where are you?" More heavy breathing. Horns blared in the background.

"I'm in the Bronx. Destiny called me. She said she needed to talk. I told her to come over. She said her friend's mother was bringin' her, so I gave her my address. But, when the car pulled up and she jumped out, Buddy was with her. He had her by the hair, coming up my stairs. And... Oh, Buddy, just get here! Hurry!" She gave me her location, before I hung up the phone.

Rayven opened her eyes just as my call was ending. "Kaleb, what's the matter, baby?" Her voice was thick with sleep. She blinked a few times and tried to focus.

"Buddy's bitch ass got Bree, Breeyonna, and Destiny. He popped Bree already. Ain't no tellin' what he about to do to Destiny. I gotta get over there and find out what's going on. Then track this nigga down and murder his bitch ass. My sister ain't got shit to do with this," I said, feeling a lump form in my throat.

I imagined him grabbing her by the hair, causing her pain, and it made me want to snap the fuck out, and break down at the same time. Destiny was only thirteen. Innocent.

Rayven held out her arms. "Give me a hug before you go. I know I can't stop you, so I ain't gon' even try. Come 'mere."

I wasn't in the mood for no lovey-dovey shit, but after what she'd done to bring our child into the world, I felt I owed her at least a hug before I got on my G-shit. Besides, I didn't know for a fact if this hug would be my last time hugging her. But, I slipped into her arms and held her close.

She tightened her grip around me. "Kaleb, I love you with all of my heart. I know you're angry right now, but you're going to have to be smart. Buddy is an idiot. A low-life. He has nothin' to lose. On top of that, he's a drug addict. That makes him dangerous. Had I thought all of this through, I would have never gotten him that attorney and paid his bail. But, we can't cry over spilled milk." She took a deep breath and hugged me even tighter. "We can pay somebody to handle this business. I hope you know that."

I slipped out of her arms. "You got this nigga a lawyer? And paid his bail? Are you serious?" I felt my temper getting hot.

"Baby, please, let's not go there. I don't want to argue you with you right now. You have a bunch of dangerous things ahead of you to accomplish. I don't want the last things we say to each other to be damaging."

"Rayven, do you have any idea what you've done? The worst thing you could possibly do, you did. You helped this nigga get back out when we are at war. Fuck, that was stupid!" I mugged her and had thoughts of snatching her ass up, but given the circumstances, that wouldn't have been smart.

"Baby, I just wanted her out of our lives. I figured if he was back out, they could reconcile and leave you out of it. They used to be so in love. I was thinking maybe they could find that spark again. I just want my husband back. That's all." Tears fell out of her eyes.

I stood there for a while, not saying a word. Just looking her over while she cried. I thought about my daughter and how she felt in my arms, then looked Rayven over

Rise to Power 2

again, and my anger subsided just enough to think rationally. Rayven had done what any woman in love would have done to get another woman out her way, so I couldn't hold it against her, as much as I wanted too.

"Baby, I can tell that you have feelings for her and it's killing me, especially now. I need you. Why can't you understand that?"

In response I rushed over and kissed her lips, then rushed out of the room. Had I stayed any longer, I would have said some things I'd regret and did not mean. I had to keep our daughter at the forefront of my brain from here on out.

\* \* \*

When I pulled up in front of the Denny's in the north side of the Bronx, I jumped out of my truck, rushed inside and found Bree sitting in the women's stall, right where we'd agreed to meet. She had a black shirt pressed up against her shoulder. It was stained with her blood. I put my arm around her and walked her outside, just as it began to rain heavily. Got her into the passenger's side and slammed the door, then rushed around to the other side.

"Yo, what the fuck happened?"

"Kaleb, you need to take me to my house. I'm not going to say nothing until you get there. Please. Let's just go." I scrunched my face and mugged her.

Lightning flashed across the sky. Thunder roared, and then it was raining so hard, it sounded like hail hitting my truck. "We gotta get you to the hospital, shorty. It looks like you're fucked up."

She started crying. Shook her head. "It's just a graze. You need to take me home. Please, I'll explain everything to you once you get there." She laid her face in her lap and started sobbing real loud. The audio made my heart drop

113

T.J. Edwards

into my stomach. I could tell that something was incredibly wrong.

"Yo, awright." I started the truck and pulled off. The whole way to her crib I kept on looking over at her. She kept the shirt pressed to her shoulder. I wondered what the matter was. I wanted to ask her so many questions, but held my tongue. When we pulled up to the spot I'd copped for her in Yonkers, I pulled my nine millimeter out of my pants, and rushed around and opened the truck door for her. She stepped out and looked into the night. The rain was pelting down on the both of us.

"Come on, Kaleb. You'll see what I'm talking about."

She jogged toward the house with me behind her. We ran along the gangway. Went in through the back door. I didn't know why she'd chosen to take that route, but I followed suit. When we got back there, the first thing I noticed was that the back door was barely hanging on by its hinges. There were splinters all over the ground. She moved it aside and it swung inward. Then, we were rushing up the stairs and into the house. She stopped and turned around to face me.

Stopping so abrupt, I bumped into her. "Kaleb, go into the den. I can't go through that again. Just go in there and tell me what we should do." She fell to her knees, looking up at me with tears streaming out of her eyes. Once again, I wanted to sit there and question her. Somethin' was most definitely up. I felt like I had the bubble guts. I swallowed and nodded at her. Took my other pistol off of my waist, and headed toward the den on high alert. The lights were off all over the house, but as I went through each room, I flicked them on. There were big footprints on the white carpet, as if a bunch of people with dirty shoes had been tracking all over the area. I kept going and when I made it to the den, my stomach flipped for the second time as soon as I got to the doorway, I felt sick. I slid my hand inside of the

114

room, searching for the light switch. When I located them, I flicked them on and looked forward. I saw her right away and fell to my knees.

T.J. Edwards

# Chapter 12

Destiny had been tied to a chair by her wrists. Somebody had sat her naked in the chair, before stabbing her all over the face and slitting her throat. Her chair sat in a pool of her own blood. Her eyes had been carved out. Blood gushed out of the sockets. The way her ankles were tied to the chair left her privates wide open and exposed. Beside her, about ten feet away by the couch, was Breeyonna's body. Her throat appeared to be cut as well. She lay on her stomach, with blood rushing out of the slit in her neck. Unlike Destiny, she still had her clothes on.

I got up from my knees and rushed to Destiny's side, attacking the binds that held her captive. Tears streaming down my face and dripping from my chin. "Destiny! Destiny! What the fuck?" I hollered, feeling weak and sick.

Bree came to the doorway and sank to her knees. Crawled over to Breeyonna and picked her up into her arms. Cradling her, before breaking down so loud I couldn't hear myself think. I undid Destiny's last bind and pulled her into my arms. Her body felt light, void of the majority of its blood. She lay limp against me, while I cried my eyes out. I couldn't believe Buddy had killed my little sister. He'd taken things way too far. Not only had he killed her, but he'd killed his own daughter as well. The nigga had to be out of his mind and I was sure to make him pay for this. Destiny came second to my mother in my heart. This was a death that would rock me for a long, long time.

I held my sister tight. Crying and crying. It had been so long since I'd released my tears into the atmosphere to purge my inner pain. Only a few hours prior, I'd shed tears over the birth of my daughter, now I was crying over the death of my sister. And though I was crazy about

Breeyonna, the loss of Destiny overpowered my feeling of sickness for Breeyonna.

"He said you tainted his daughter. That you ruined our family. He said he's going to destroy your family like you did his. That's when he shot at me and tried to kill me. Had I not jumped out of the bedroom window, he would have killed me like he told me he was going to do them. I didn't know if he'd done it for real until right now. What are we going to do? What are we going to do?" she whimpered, rocking back and forth with Breeyonna's dead body.

So many images of my sister growing up flashed through my head. Images of me buying her, her first pair of Jordans. Then Timbs. All the dresses. Teaching her how to ride a bike. Her crying over my shoulder when her first boyfriend broke her heart and started to mess with her best friend. Holding her. Her kisses. I'd promised to take her out on a date so we could spend some time together. I wanted to spend some money on her. Spoil her. Treat her as a princess, just so she could know that she was special. Now, she was gone. No longer breathing. I was so sick, I picked her up and carried her to the bathroom, where I purged my guts into the toilet. Once I was able to peel myself away from the toilet, I curled up on the bathroom floor with her body and held her. All I could do was cry.

* * *

The next afternoon, I had an ounce of heroin in front of me. I separated into thin lines, taking them one by one. I was on my eighth line, high as a kite. Bree sat across from me on the sofa, just as high. Some time that morning, she'd told me she'd lost our child and had been afraid to tell me. That was too much for me. The bodies of Breeyonna and Destiny laid on the side of the couch, swelling up already because of how hot we had the house.

"I'm finna find that bitch-ass nigga, and kill every nigga he wit. Word is bond. I'ma 'bout to knock this pussy's head off. That's on my mother!" I hollered and tooted a line hard.

I tilted my head back and absorbed my high. I was shaking. My heart beating so fast I could barely breathe. The pain in my soul was slowly subsiding, that was until I looked down and saw Destiny's body laid out. Bree knelt in front of the table.

"I'm hurting Kaleb. I can't believe my baby is gone. What am I going to do? She was all I had, besides you." She tooted a line so hard, she started to cough. Sat back against the sofa and beat on her chest with her little fist, then broke into tears again.

"Yo, it's good, Bree. Word is bond, my cousins on the way up here from Chicago as we speak. Bruh 'nem get down like I get down. Buddy think shit sweet, yo, it's kill season. Mufucka killed my sister, it's kill season, Bree. That's my word!" More tears fell from my eyes. I slid off of the couch and cuddled up with my sister's body again.

I still couldn't believe she was gone, and I didn't know what I was going to tell my mother. I knew Destiny's death would break her, especially when she found out how she'd been murdered, and by whom. I wasn't prepared for her reaction. Bree's eyes were low. She crawled across the floor and gathered Breeyonna into her arms.

She kissed her forehead and began to rock back and forth with her again. "What kind of man would do this to his own child? How sick do you have to be to do something like this, Kaleb?" She snuggled her face into the crook of Breeyonna's neck and cried her eyes out. "I'm so sorry, baby. Mama so sorry. I should have never let him get close to you. It's my fault. It's all my fault. I hate me right now. I won't ever get over it. I just won't. Oh Lord, why? Why, Father?"

She looked toward the ceiling and pleaded with God for an explanation. I wasn't thinking about getting a response for the man upstairs. My mind was set on how many niggas I was about to send to him. I was feeling murderous. Cold blooded and ready to see blood. I couldn't wait until my cousins touched down. I was expecting their flight to land at JFK later that night. I had already sent both of them first-class tickets and told them the matter was urgent. Even though our relationship wasn't the closest, my cousins had a knack for killing shit. The times I had visited them in Chicago in my teens during the summers, they stayed in beef. In fact, I committed my first murder in Chicago while with them. Bree whimpered as she held Breeyonna. I looked down at Destiny and shook my head. What the fuck was I going to tell my mother?

\* \* \*

Ajani walked circles around Destiny's body, with a mug on his face. He was five feet eight inches tall and real muscular. He had a short haircut, with deep waves. Caramel-skinned and real handsome. One of those pretty-boy types with a lethal temper. He was my aunt's second-born son. He knelt in front of Destiny. "Cuz, I never liked that bitch nigga, Buddy. I knew one day we was gon' have to get up wit his glamour." He kissed Destiny on the forehead and shook his head, before standing up. "I'm sorry, Rayjon couldn't make it. That nigga handling some other shit with his bitch. He said he'll be out here in a few days, but I wouldn't bank on it. But I'm here and I'm ready to set the city on fire. We can meet up wit my niggas over in Jersey for a few minutes, then roll back out this way and sweat somethin'. I can give them niggas a few birds and they gon' crush everything on sight." He pulled his nose. "May I?"

he asked and nodded his head toward the table that had the platters of heroin on 'em.

I nodded and knelt beside Destiny. "Gon' 'head. I gotta break the news to my mother." I took my phone out of my pocket and pulled up her number, ready to dial it.

Ajani tooted a line, and threw his head back, pinching his nose. "Damn, Joe, that shit strong as hell," he said through a strained voice. There was a thick vein that appeared on the side of his neck. He coughed and tried to swallow his spit, before I handed him the bottle of apple juice that was sitting on the table. I had been drinking it earlier. It had been the only thing I'd been able to keep down, and even it made me gag. I was sick over Destiny's heinous murder. After drinking half of the bottle, Ajani put it down. His eyes were bloodshot and low. "You go ahead and tell her what's good, J. Let her know I'm in town, and she gon' already know what it is. She know her sister, Jersey, got some lunatics for sons." He sat on the couch and pulled out his phone. "After you holler at her, we gotta handle these bodies, and take a drive out to Camden." I exhaled loudly and shook my head. Walked into the back of the house with my phone, I didn't know how I was going to break things to my mother. I got to thinking it would have been smarter to holler at her in person. That way, if she broke down like I was expecting her to do, I would be there to comfort and console her. I was having a hard time keeping it together and my mother was already more unglued than I was, from worrying about my sister the way she was.

Bree came into the living room where I stood with my back turned, lost in thought. She placed her hand on my shoulder. It had dried-up blood on it. "Baby, I think you should just go to her and tell her in person. This isn't the type of thing you should tell somebody over the phone. It'll do way more damage that way. Trust me." She walked around to face me. Took my hands into hers. Looked into my eyes and blinked back tears. "I don't know how we're going to get through this, but we are. As long as we have each other." Her face scrunched. She broke into a fit of tears. "Buddy can't get away with this. He just can't. You have to find him, Kaleb. Find him and make him pay for what he's done to our babies." She wrapped her arms around me and broke down against me. "I hate him so much," she wailed.

\* \* \*

My mother walked backward, shaking her head. "No. No. Don't tell me that, Kaleb. No, she's not. No, my baby is not dead. Please don't tell me that." She screamed and sunk to the floor on her butt. Buried her face into her lap and started sobbing so loud, two nurses ran into the room on high alert.

"Is everything okay in here?" a short, heavyset black woman asked, looking from my mother then up to me.

I shook my head. "We've had a death in the family. We need a moment to grieve. Please." I led them out of the room. Closed the door, then sunk down beside my mother. Placed my arm around her small body and pulled her to me.

"Come here, baby. I know you're hurting right now, but we have to get through this. My sister is in a better place. We have to believe that. We can never question God's plan. Remember, you taught me that?" She buried her face in my under arm and cried as loud as she could, while balling my clothes into her fists. The more she cried, the sicker it made me. I never liked to hear my mother cry. Never liked to know she was in any form of pain. My mother was my queen. I didn't love anybody nearly as much as I did her. She shook her head and looked up at me with tears running down her cheek.

## Rise to Power 2

"How did she go? What happened, son? Please. Tell me the truth, no lies." I helped her come to her feet. Led her to her bed and sat her on the end of it. I wiped her tears away with my thumbs and kissed her on the forehead. Took a deep breath and tried to decide in my head if I was going to give her the raw version, or if I was going to edit it a lot. Growing up, something my mother never did was to shield us from the uncut truth. She gave it to us just as it was, and I knew she expected the same from me right then. I had never lied to my mother for as long as I could remember, and I wasn't about to pick this day to start. "It was Buddy. He slit Destiny's throat and stabbed her a bunch of times in the face. On top of that, he killed little Breeyonna, too and left both of them in Bree's house. It's sick."

Her eyes got bucked. She looked off and covered her mouth. "He slit her throat? Buddy. The kid I watched grow up from a little boy? Why would he do this to us, Kaleb? Why? Is it because of you getting his hand cut off?" she asked.

I shrugged my shoulders. "It could be that or a bunch of other stuff. Bruh doing heroin now, real tough. His mind has been clouded for a minute. He tried to kill Bree before he did this to them. That fool just need his head knocked off. Ajani just flew in from Chicago today. We about to ride out to New Jersey and mount up. Get a couple of the killas from out there to come back to New York with us, so we can find Buddy and send him to the Reaper. That nigga gotta pay for what he did to Destiny. Ain't no way around that."

My mother got up from the bed and shook her head. "You fucking that girl, ain't you?" She said this, looking back over her shoulder at me. Then, she turned all the way around to face me. I hung my head and kept silent. I didn't know what to say 'cause I knew what she was getting at. My mother was trying to make sense of things in her head, and no matter what she did, all fingers were going to come back pointing at me.

"Yeah, I was hitting her on a regular. I don't think Buddy knew that though. But, then again, I can't be too sure."

She frowned and more tears dropped out of her eyes. "So, this is what he does to my child, because of some girl both of y'all are fucking? This ain't right. It ain't right, Kaleb, and you know it." She rushed into the bathroom and slammed the door. "You and Ajani better find his ass and do what you gotta do. Drop my baby's body off with Mr. O'Bee in Harlem. I'ma give her a nice funeral. It's the least I can do since I couldn't protect her." Then, she was sobbing so loud, I had to get out of the room before I broke down.

# Chapter 13

"Yo, Ajani, you already know we riding wit you god, word up. If we gotta roll out to the NY to heat some niggas, then it is what it is. Just tell us where and when?" the tall dark-skinned man said with a red rag hanging out the right side of his pocket.

He had five-point stars all over his face and neck. We were seated down in the basement of an apartment complex in Camden, New Jersey, a few blocks away from The Peter McGuire Gardens. The basement had ten other niggas down there besides me, Ajani, and this dark-skinned stud. All of them had big handles hanging out of their waist-bands. They looked grimy, with long dread locks or bald heads. Their eyes were on the table, where Ajani had placed two kilos of pure cocaine.

Ajani pushed the dope over to the dark-skinned dude. "I'ma 'bout to roll out with my cousin right now. Once we find out where this nigga is located, it's going down. I'll hit you up ASAP, Blood. Yo ass betta be ready to go. This seventy-two ounces is just a down payment for the up and coming bloodshed. Nah' mean? I ain't fucked wit you in a minute, but I know it's all love and then some. This shit ninety percent too. Don't get no better. Try me out."

The dark-skinned nigga grabbed one of the birds and stuck a Swiss Army knife into it. It came up with a pinch of cocaine on its tip. He placed it to his nostril and snorted it off of the blade, stuck the kilo again and tooted some up the other nostril. Leaned back with a big smile on his face, after waiting for the effects of the coke to kick in. "Damn, Slime, this what the fuck I been waiting on. My plug just got knocked on a humbug. The family been starving for a few weeks now, but now that the god back in town, I can bank on us having something on the table every night. Nah' mean?" he sucked his teeth and looked over his shoulder at his troops. Ajani mugged him and then mugged his crew.

"Ain't shit free, niggas. When I feed the masses, it's because I'm looking for somethin' in return. That's blood-shed. My aunt in the hospital fighting against cancer, and now she just found out that her only daughter has been mur-dered by a low-life dope head. I ain't honoring that shit. I'm ready to paint New York red on behalf of my beloveds. If my pops ain't just get knocked, y'all already know how Greed would've come through this bitch. He ain't a legend for nothing." Ajani wiped his mouth and continued to mug them.

"I'd heard stories about my uncle Greed all while grow-ing up. He was supposed to have been a major nigga in the game. He ran a crew of savages that were called the Ski Mask Cartel. They were deadly and relentless. Some of the older heads in New York made a movie about my uncle Greed's crew called *Bloody Commas.* I had only met him a few times and each time, I felt the presence of death loom-ing around him." The dark-skinned nigga mugged Ajani back.

"I ain't never been one to accept no handouts. These two kilos and the promise of you being my plug for six months a be enough for me and my Bloods to go ape shit like the Carters, all over New York. You just do what you gotta do and it's a wrap. That's on my veins, nigga." He smacked his forearm.

Ajani turned his head sideways. Looked him up and down, then rose from the table. "Then ain't shit else left to be said. Fuck wit me, and I'ma help you flood Camden just like old times. I'm still plugged like electricity. Know that."

\*\*\*

# Rise to Power 2

I tooted me a few lines of heroin, because I was starting to feel sick. The drug was fucking wit my body in a way I didn't want it too. I wouldn't say I was addicted, but it was to the point where if I didn't treat my nose, I was getting a severe headache, and feeling like I was about to throw up. My stomach felt as if it were in knots. As soon as I tooted the poison, I was back feeling lovely. The endorphins in my brain were firing on all cylinders and I could think straight. I felt golden. Lifted. Ready to kill up some shit. Ajani pulled a sharp ass hunting knife out of his inside coat pocket. He looked it over while I drove my truck.

"Yo, anybody can smoke a nigga, Cuz. But, when you really, really want to kill a nigga, you gotta use one of these bitches right here. The feel of this steel tearing through muscles and tissue is like no other. It's like fucking without a rubber after strapping up with one for so long." He slid it back into his inside sheath. "Yo, you really think these niggas gon' know where this fool hiding out at?" he asked, looking over at me.

"Braylen is his closest cousin. Even though kid ain't in these streets like that, Buddy always fuck wit him and let him know what's good. So, if anybody knows where he is, it's him." I said getting off of the expressway in East New York.

I kept seeing visions of Buddy with his throat slit in my head. Saw the blood rushing out of his neck and everything. I wanted that fuck nigga dead. Couldn't believe he iced Destiny and Breeyonna like he had. "I'm letting you know right now, Kaleb. I'm from Chicago, nigga, that means I'm a Windy City Kid. We don't give a fuck about killing bitches, kids, or old people, none of that shit. Right now, I'm in my fucking zone, Blood. All I care about is death. When we get over here, don't look to put no leash on me. Son, you do that and we gon' have a major problem.

Straight up. I ain't come all the way out here to play games." He drank from the apple juice in the console.

I scoffed. "Nigga, you acting like we don't get down out here. I'm a Harlem nigga. All we do is get money and commit murders with no remorse. You niggas down in Chicago kill just for the fun of it," I said, fucking wit him. I knew that would irritate him. He was Chicago crazy and had been, even as a shorty.

"For blocks, nigga. We kill to take over blocks that gross major money. It ain't for nothing. Mufuckas gangbang too, but I just bang for my family. I'ma Edwards. It's Ski Mask Cartel until I die, word up." I remained silent and pulled up into the back of Braylen's project building twenty minutes later. He stayed on the tenth floor of the Red Hook Houses. Lucky for me, I had a few niggas I sold weight to that ran the building. So, when security saw my face, instead of them questioning me about what I was doing over there, or patting me and Ajani down, they let us roll through after getting the nod from one of my buyers that ran that portion of the building we were trying to travel through.

The Red Hook Houses were grimy, and filthy on the inside. There was trash all over the hallways, and they reeked of piss and feces. There were heroin addicts all over the place, shooting up on the stairwells, and even freaking each other. Big rats ran along the walls, and almost every apartment we walked past was blarin' their music loud. This didn't bother me and it actually helped me and Ajani to do what we needed to do.

When I got in front of Braylen's apartment, I placed my ear on the door to see if I could hear any noise on the other side. As soon as I heard a few male voices, I nodded at Ajani and took a step back, then with all of my might, kicked in the door right by the lock. It flew in. Ajani rushed alongside of me into the apartment, with both of his guns out. Without even saying a word, he got to squeezing his triggers. The guns were equipped with silencers, so the only noise I heard was the dudes crying out in pain as his bullets slammed into their backs and legs.

*Poof! Poof! Poof! Poof!* More fire spit from his guns and there were two dudes laying on the living room floor, crawling with holes in their backs. They strained and struggled to breathe. Ajani stomped them in the back of the neck and finished them off with multiple shots to their heads. Blood splattered onto the carpet. Braylen was on his knees in the kitchen with his hands in the air, shaking his head from right to left. There were heroin works all over the floor. No table or refrigerator. Just him and a bunch of roaches crawling everywhere.

"Please, I don't know what's going on, but I swear to God I ain't got no money in here. All I got is seven grams of dope. You can have it," he said, looking at the kitchen floor.

I flipped the gun on safety, turned it around and slammed the handle into his forehead, planting a huge hole right in the middle of it. Then grabbed him by the throat and picked him up, forcing him into the wall.

"Where the fuck is Buddy hiding out at?" I cocked the hammer and pressed the barrel into the hole already in his forehead. Twisting it a bit to cause pain.

"Argh! Man, oh fuck, Kaleb. Man, I swear I don't know what Buddy did to you, but I ain't have nothing to do wit it. Why are you doing me like this, man?" he asked, with his breath smelling like raw sewage.

On top of that he was musty, smelling like ass. I kneed him in the nuts, picked him up and slammed him to the floor. I was heated because I felt he was about to give me the runaround. I ain't have time for that or his games, period. I wanted Buddy's ass, and I wanted it now.

## T.J. Edwards

Blood oozed into his eyes and ran into his mouth. "Nigga, I ain't telling you shit. You out of order for fucking his bitch and calling them pigs on him. Real niggas don't get down like that. So do what you gotta do, fuck nigga." He swung and connected with my jaw, catching me off guard.

It dazed me, but I bounced back real fast. I took the pistol and smacked him across the face with it, once, twice, then five times in a row. His blood splattered all over the kitchen walls. He moaned in pain every time the steel crashed into the bones of his face. But, I kept on beating him senseless. Harder and harder, with no mercy. Beat him until Ajani pulled me off of him.

Braylen was crawling around on the floor with his face leaking. His teeth were everywhere. He struggled to breathe. Coughed and spit up big globs of bright red mucus. Ajani grabbed him by the shirt and dragged him into the living room. Pulled out his knife and straddled him.

"Look, I ain't gon play these games wit you, home boy. You either gon' tell me what we need to know, or I'm about to slice you up like deep dish pizza, Chicago-style. Let's get the ball rolling." He slashed him across the face three quick times, then slammed the knife into his shoulder so hard, it sunk all the way to the handle.

Braylen hollered at the top of his lungs. The gashes in his face were oozing. His legs kicked into the air. He tried to hump Ajani off of him with no success. "I ain't gon' ask you again, my nigga. You got ten seconds to tell us what's good."

Braylen inhaled sharply and swallowed. "I don't give a fuck what you niggas do. It's death before dishonor wit me, Blood." He snorted as hard as he could and got ready to blow a loogey into Ajani's face. But, Ajani must have saw it coming, because he raised the knife as far as he could into the air, and slammed it into Braylen's throat, jugging

130

him. Pulled it out and slammed it back in a second time, and pulled it upward ripping a big divide in his throat. Blood rushed out of it and all over Ajani's right hand. He stood up and wiped the knife on Braylen's shirt.

"Bitch-ass nigga had heart. I liked that shit. I can see that being back in New York about to be fun as hell. All I need in the moment is a few strippers, and some more of that good shit you had me sniffing on earlier. Get yo ducks in a row, Kaleb. We gon' find this nigga, trust me." I looked down on Braylen with my chest heaving up and down. I didn't know how I was going to find Buddy, but I had to come up with a plan real fast.

* * *

Bree slid in the bed next to me and laid her head on my chest. I had my eyes wide open, looking at the ceiling in the dark. Visions of Braylen's corpse kept going through my mind. Then Destiny's, and Breeyonna's. I was feeling sick and hadn't eaten a meal in nearly four days. I couldn't keep anything down. Every time it went into my mouth, I gagged. I was starting to lose weight and become physically sick.

We'd dropped Destiny and Breeyonna's bodies to O'Bee's funeral home and paid him to keep our matter quiet. The last thing we needed was a bunch of New York City dicks sniffing around, asking questions, delaying us from seeking street justice. My family didn't want the cops involved. It wasn't how we got down. We believed in handling our own bidness. I wanted to murder Buddy myself and witness the life leaving out of his body. It was the only thing that could have eased my pain.

"Baby, I see her face every time I blink. It's making me sick. I don't know how to deal with this," she said, shivering. She snuggled closer to me.

I shook my head. "I know, baby. This shit is killing me too. I keep seeing my sister and Breeyonna. This nigga gotta pay for this shit. Ain't no way I'm about to let this ride. The only way I'ma feel better is when I know he laying six feet deep, after I have fun wit his bitch ass. Those were two perfect princesses. Goddesses. They had bright futures. I was gon' make sure of that. Now they're gone and all because of what? Man, I hate that bitch-ass nigga." I slammed my fist on the bed and slid out of her embrace. I started to pace back and forth with my head down. My stomach growled. I felt dizzy. My vision blurry. "It's my fault, Bree. I let this shit happen to those babies. I did this. I'll never be able to live wit myself."

I walked over to the dresser and pulled out the top drawer. Took my dope out of it, and came and placed it on the night table beside our bed. Knelt, and made four thin lines. I needed the emotional pain to stop hurting me. Needed to feel stronger. The heroin would help with this, I was sure of that. I picked up the straw and placed it inside of my nostril before snorting a line hard.

As soon as the drug entered into my system, it was like my brain exploded. The high took me up into the clouds. My entire body got numb. Emotionally, I was unable to feel down. I could only feel a sense of euphoria. Happy, even though I knew I wasn't supposed to. I tried to fight the feeling, but I knew that I needed it. I was hurting too bad. I kept imagining how it felt to hold Destiny in my arms the last time we were at the hospital and she fell asleep in my arms. I wished I could go back in time. I would never let her climb from my lap. Knowing what I know now, I would still be holding her. Holding her as tight as I could. I would never let her go, I thought, before breaking into tears.

Bree climbed out of the bed and rubbed my back. Kissed my cheek. "Baby, we're going to get through this. This is us. There is nothing we can't overcome together."

She wrapped her arms around my neck and pulled me into her embrace again.

As angry as I felt, her embrace was what I needed. I needed to be held by a woman. A woman that I cared about. One that was going through the same pain that I was. I had never felt more connected to Bree. I felt like I needed her more than ever. Only she could understand my pain. "I love you so much, Kaleb. I love you with all of my heart. It sucks we have to go through this, but I wouldn't want to go through this with anyone other than you. You are my rock." She kissed my cheek, and then my neck. She wiggled all the way in front of me and kissed my lips. Sliding her tongue all over mines.

Our kiss was loud and very much needed. The drug had me fully aroused. My penis stuck up against my pajama pants. Throbbing. She backed up and took ahold of it in her fist. Pulled it out of the pants and pumped it up and down.

"We need to take our minds off this tragedy, baby. Please let's just do this. Anything but to sit here and think about them every second of the night. Please." She licked her lips, then lowered her head into my lap. She took my dick hungrily into her mouth, making my toes curl.

I grabbed a handful of her hair and started to slowly hump her mouth. I tried my best not to see Destiny and Breeyonna. I tried so hard not focus on the fact that Buddy was still alive, laying in the weeds, waiting to attack us off guard. I just wanted to enjoy the pleasure Bree was providing. "That shit feel so good, baby. Suck that dick for daddy. Take my mind away from this bullshit, I got you next. I swear, I do."

She moaned around my pole and started to suck me faster and faster. I didn't know what was going through her mind, but I could only imagine it was similar to what was going on inside of mine. How could it not be?

133

## T.J. Edwards

She popped my dick out and pulled her gown over her head, exposing her naked body underneath. Even though I was sick and angry, I couldn't deny how sexy her body was. It looked amazing. As the drug coursed through my veins and heightened my level of sexual desire, my need for her increased.

She stood up and slid her fingers through her slit. Rubbing it up and down. "Come on, daddy. Please. I need you to fuck me to take me away from this pain. I can't take this shit." Tears came out of her eyes as she backed up and fell on the bed. She opened her thick thighs wide and summoned me.

I stood up and wiped my face. Kicked my pants all the way off and got between her legs. I took ahold of my dick and ran it up and down her hot crease, until she became so wet that it was leaking out of her. She started to cry harder. Squeezing her eye lids together. "Daddy, please heal me. Please. I miss my baby so much."

I humped forward and slid deep into her body. Began working my pole in and out, while she dug her nails into my shoulder blades. "Bree. I need you. I need you, boo. Aw. Baby. This. Shit. Hurt so bad." I started to pound her out. Cocking my back, then slamming forward on bidness. Her pussy felt hotter than usual. Her nails digging into my back, added to my pleasure. You couldn't have pleasure without pain. The perfect combination for me. It was exactly what I needed. I needed her.

"Huh! Harder, Kaleb! Harder! I need you to fuck me as hard as you can! Uh! I can take it, baby! I can take it!" She threw her head back and cried harder. Wrapped her legs around my waist and tried to sit up, hugging me while I dug into her body deeper and deeper. With every stroke, my love for her grew.

Images of both Destiny and Breeyonna tore into my mind. No matter how hard I tried, I could not stop seeing them. And, because I was, it made it hard for me to maintain an erection, but I kept going. Kept going until my piece withered, and lay limp against my thigh. I fell to the side of Bree, who was already sobbing and repeating how much she missed Breeyonna.

T.J. Edwards

## Chapter 14

We had Destiny's and Breeyonna's funerals ten days later. Because their bodies were in such a horrible state, the mortician had needed more time to work with both of them, and there was no way we could argue with him. We decided to have the service inside the funeral home, instead of the church. Ajani had his hittas from Camden County act as security. They sealed off the perimeter around the funeral home, and a few of them even patrolled up and down the block while the service was going on. This was rough for me, because both Bree and Rayven were there.

Rayven was taking Destiny's murder just as hard as Derez, and my mother and me. She'd broken down and slid to the floor three times, within the first hour of the ceremony, while Bree on the other side of the aisle was breaking down horribly. She had a few of her family members over there to support her, but I could tell she was longing for me to wrap her in my arms and that made me sick. I wrapped my arm around my mother's shoulders and led her to Destiny's casket. Both caskets were at the front of the funeral home, side by side. It was so sad, I could not stop shedding tears. When my mother made it to her coffin, she leaned over it and laid her face on Destiny's chest. She was dressed in a pink and white Prada dress, with her curly hair flowing over her shoulders.

The mortician had done all he could to stitch and put make-up over the knife wounds in her face. Every time I looked down at her, I got sick on the stomach. I still couldn't believe my baby sister was gone. That Buddy had taken her away from our family. My mother smoothed out Destiny's dress. Touched her hair, then rubbed the side of her cheek. Tears dropped from her eyes. She shook her head and looked up at the ceiling of the funeral home as if she saw the face of God.

"I don't understand why you took my baby, Father. You took her at thirteen. She was so young. So full of life. I just don't get it." She kissed Destiny on the forehead. Stepped over to Breeyonna's casket and shook her head again. "This baby didn't even have a chance to get her life started. It's just not fair. She kissed Breeyonna's little cheeks and said a short prayer over her. Then, side-stepped back to Destiny's coffin. Looked her over for a few minutes and broke into tears. I rubbed her back, tears coming down my cheeks as well.

Bree slid behind me and rested her hand on my shoulder. "Kaleb, would you mind if I said a few words to your mother?" She looked into my eyes, after taking her Chanel glasses off of her face.

I shook my head. "Nall, it's good. I'm pretty sure she needs to hear some encouraging words right now."

She smiled weakly and rubbed my mother's back. "Ma'am, I am sorry for your loss. I will keep you and your family in my prayers. I know exactly what you're feeling."

She went in for a hug, but my mother stepped backward and mugged her. "Bitch, don't try to hug me. This is partially your fault. You knew damn well what kind of man you were dealing with. You should have known something like this was going to take place. Buddy was crazy over your little shapely ass."

Bree looked appalled. "Excuse me? Are you trying to say this was my fault?" she asked with her voice breaking up.

My mother scrunched her face and stepped closer into Bree's. "Clean out your ears little girl, I said partially. You should have known better than to be fucking my son. He was Buddy's best friend. All these dudes in Harlem, but you had to get in between two home boys. If that ain't the definition of a thot, then I don't know what is."

She gave her a disgusted look. Bree gasped, and bucked her eyes like she couldn't believe my mother was coming at her like that. I think she failed to realize my mother was from the slums of Port Au Prince, Haiti. She left those slums and settled into the slums of Harlem. So, though she may have been years older than us, she was still as hood as they came. And honest.

Bree looked down into her gray eyes and swallowed. "Look, I don't know what you're talking about? Or how you even know that much, but I'll tell you this, I love your son. I haven't screwed or messed around with Buddy since me and Kaleb laid down together. I fell in love with Kaleb because he was always cleanin' up Buddy's messes. Buddy never cared about me, or his daughter. Case in point." She nodded at Breeyonna's coffin with her head. "Your son and I were boyfriend and girlfriend way before Buddy came along. That's a fact."

"Nall, bitch, the fact is that my daughter is laying here in a casket, because you couldn't keep your fucking thighs closed. Pussy has always been the one downfall that splits up crews and gets people killed. I don't care what you guys' back story is, the bottom line is that it is toxic. If I wasn't as sick as I am right now, and hopped up off of these morphine pills the doctors gave me, I'd kick yo ass like your mother should be doing right now. Stay away from my son before you get him killed next." She looked into her eyes, giving her a menacing stare. It was like steam was coming off the top of her head.

"Ma, chill. It ain't her fault. Buddy ain't got a clue of what me and Bree been doing. Son just got issues. He ain't right. Any nigga that a slump their own daughter ain't right in the head. And as far as her staying away from me, nah, that ain't gon' happen. I got mad love for Bree. She in my heart real tough. I'ma hold her down. Ain't none of this her fault. I came at her. I told her what it was gon' be and she put up a fight for a little while, but in the end, I prevailed. So, if you gon' blame what happened to Destiny and Breeyonna on anybody, you can take your anger out on me."

*Smack*! She hit me so hard that I spit my gum into the front pew. "Cool. I ain't got no problem doing that, since you wanna play Captain Save-A-Ho. Well, since you gon' choose to keep messin' around with this heathen, just keep her away from me, or I'll draw up a spell so foul she'll be chasing her own tail. I don't like you, lil girl. I don't trust you. And, I don't want no parts of you, or the curses that follow you. If you're anywhere around me when I get healthy, I'm going to put Vaseline all over my face before I take you out in the middle of the street and kick your ass. Do you hear me?" She bumped her hard and stepped past her. Mugging her the whole time. Even sucked her teeth, before walking off, mumbling to herself.

Bree stood dumbfounded and noticeably hurt. She turned to me and came over, hugging the lower portion of my body. Behind us, the funeral home's guests were talking amongst themselves, or watching us. The choir from our church was setting themselves up in the corner of the funeral home. I saw Rayven hand our daughter to my mother, then she was coming across the room with her Gucci shades on her face. She took Bree's arm and pulled it off of me.

"Bitch, get yo hands off of my fiancé. You better take yo ass over there and hug up with one of your relatives," she snapped. I could see the tear streaks in the foundation of her make-up.

Bree took a deep breath and balled up her fists. "Yo, don't touch me like that, Rayven. Today ain't the day, ma, trust me on that." She stepped up to me. "Kaleb, I'm about to go over here and chill. I don't feel like fighting nobody on my daughter's burial day." She kissed me on the cheek and turned to walk back to her seat.

"Aw, hell nall." Rayven dropped her glasses to the carpet and pushed Bree in the back so hard, she went stumbling into the choir. Two of the females fell on top of her.

"Bitch, I told you to keep your body parts to yourself. But, I see I'ma have to teach you a lesson. Word."

"That's right, baby. Kick her ass. Lord knows if I could, I would. That girl is trifling," my mother hollered. Then my daughter burst into tears.

Bree made it to her feet and shook her head. "You know what, Rayven, bring it on. I'm not scared of you. I whooped your ass once in middle school, and I ain't got no problem doing it as an adult. Let's get it." She rushed toward Rayven.

I rushed to separate them, when Ajani grabbed me. "Nigga, hell nall. You already know what it is. Let these bitches get out they frustrations. It ain't gon' hurt nobody." He had me bear hugged from the back. That position alone made me feel real weird, so I yanked up out of his embrace and pushed his ass.

Rayven rushed Bree, swinging wildly. Bree held her guards and protected her chin. She blocked Rayven's first two blows, side-stepped her and then gave her two shots to the jaw, grabbed her hair and yanked her to the carpet. Jumped back. "Get up, bitch. You talking all that smack. Comin' at me at my daughter's funeral and shit. Let's get it."

Rabbit rushed from the audience and tackled Bree into the drum set of the choir. The collision was so loud that everybody ran to one side of the church in a hurry, watching from a distance. Nobody made a move to break up the fight. *Welcome to Harlem*, I thought. "Get the fuck off of me, Ajani. And, don't be calling them out of their names.

T.J. Edwards

Both of them carried my seed, Blood. Word up." I rushed across the room.

By the time I got there, Bree was on top of Rabbit, punching her with one blow after the next. Rabbit's nose was bleeding all over her face. She was begging for Bree to stop. That's when Rayven rushed her and kicked her in the back. Bree rolled off of Rabbit onto her side, groaning in pain. Rayven took this as a sign to attack her ass and came once again, swinging wildly. Her fists connected with Bree's jaw, eye and chin, knocking her to the ground. She struggled to get up. Both Rabbit and Rayven began to stomp her. Rayven kept hollering something about Harlem, while Rabbit said the Bronx too many times.

Bree curled into a ball, protecting her head. I rushed over and got in front of them, moved them backward. "Y'all chill this shit out. Fuck! This a funeral. This girl lost her fucking daughter, Rayven, damn! And Rabbit, you lucky she rescued yo ass or you'd a been ass out," I snapped, pulling Bree behind me.

"Kaleb, if you don't watch yo mouth, I swear to God I'ma have another child resting with Jehovah. You need to take that lil girl up out of here before something else pop off. Don't nobody want her here. Her damn family done ran out of the door, leaving her to fend for herself. That should tell you what kind of cloth she's cut from," my mother said, bouncing my daughter up and down in her arms, patting her butt.

"Yeah, it's good, Kaleb. Just let me kiss my baby girl one more time and I'm out of here. I see what it is." She wiped a lone tear from her eye. Her nose leaked a hint of blood. Her make-up was smudged. They'd managed to pull out one of her tracks as well. I felt sorry for her. Like I should have done more.

"Gon' 'head, ma. I ain't about to let nobody else put they mittens on you. All of this is foul to begin with."

142

# Rise to Power 2

Bree slowly stepped away from me, and over to Breeyonna's coffin. She broke down looking at her. Bent all the way over the casket, placing kisses all over her face. "I love you, baby. Mama love you so much and I'm sorry. I'm sorry I couldn't protect you from that evil man. Please forgive me. Please forgive me." She picked Breeyonna up and held her in her arms.

This choked me up horribly. To witness a mother have to go through that was too much for me. I wish I could have erased all of Bree's pain. Wished she didn't have to go through that. I hated myself for not protecting both Destiny and Breeyonna.

I looked into the pews. My mother had tears coming out of her eyes. I could tell that the scene was choking her up as well. She came over with my daughter in her arms and handed her to me. "Huh, baby, I can't let her leave feeling like she feels."

She stepped over to Bree and rubbed her back. Then kissed her cheek, before they hugged and cried, holding one another. Both mothers going through the pains of what the loss of a child feels like. They had an unspoken bond and didn't even know it until they embraced each other.

Rayven stepped up to me and sniffled. "I'm sorry, Kaleb. I just can't stand to see another woman putting her hands on you. You're going to be my husband. That makes you my property, not hers. I know your mother giving in and all of that good shit, but I ain't going. My word, I feel like putting some bread up, and making sure I ain't never gotta deal with her ever again." She looked past my shoulder to see my mother and Bree hugging each other. I could tell the sight made her nervous. She saw Bree as a threat, and maybe she should have. "I know you love this bitch, Kaleb. I can sense it. She's going to be the death of you. I ain't about to lose you to nobody. I don't give a fuck who they are. I'll—."

## T.J. Edwards

"Say kid, a truck full of dread heads just pulled up outside and son, 'nem got them choppahs in their hands. Everybody move to the back of the funeral home," the dark-skinned nigga from Camden said. Ajani told me his name was Pyrex. He took two pistols out of his waistband and looked toward Ajani.

Ajani rushed to my mother's side. "Come on Auntie, let me get you to the back of this joint before any clapping start. It seem like—"

*Boom. Boom. Boom. Boom.*

The windows in the funeral home shattered. People started to scream and drop to the floor as rapid bullets were sent onto the funeral home. I rushed to Bree and grabbed Rayven's hand, running toward the back of the funeral home and into one of the rooms, where the mortician was prepping another body. The woman's body was laid out on a slab of metal, inches away from a sink. The girls ran inside, breathing hard, along with my mother and daughter. Then more people started to come into the room as well, but I didn't give a fuck about them, I was concerned about my people. Derez cut through the crowd and shielded our mother. More gunshots wrecked the funeral home.

"Look, y'all stay right here. Don't nobody come out of here until I come and get you. Y'all hear me?" I hollered at the top of my lungs. Taking both .40 Glocks from my holsters and cocking them one at a time, I grabbed the funeral home director by his suit coat. "You got a back door, Blood?"

He nodded, shaken up. "Yeah, just down the stairs. It leads to the back yard." He pointed. More shots sounded. I could hear things falling over in the front of the establishment. I prayed it wasn't one of the princess's coffins. Before I could jog away, Bree grabbed me and hugged me with all of her might.

"I love you, Kaleb. Please be careful," she begged.

# Rise to Power 2

Rayven frowned and tried to make her way across the crowded room, but I took off running as fast as I could.

*\*\*\**

I got to the back door and kicked it outward. I rushed into the back yard, hopped the fence and found myself in somebody's back yard. I ran along the side of their house as I heard more and more gunfire. When I came out of the gangway, I peeked around the porch, and saw the black Chevy Astro van parked in front of the funeral home. The side door was wide open. The shooters, three of them, stood on the grass of the funeral home, airing it out with AK-47s. The rifles had long banana clips hanging out of them. Two of Ajani's boys were laying in the grass with blood leaking out of them. I couldn't tell if they were dead or alive. What baffled me was the fact that the shooting was taking place on a busy street as if it were the most natural thing in the world. In the passenger's seat of the Astro van was a dark-skinned man with thick, long, nappy dread locks. He puffed on a cigar and blew the smoke out of the window. I nodded, curled my lip, and wit my heart beating faster than a sprinter's at the Olympics, rushed from the side of the house, shooting at the shooters.

*Blocka. Blocka. Blocka. Blocka.*

I watched one of my bullets slam into one of the shooter's necks, and buss it open. He jerked and fell face first to the grass, kicking his legs wildly. The other shooters ran for cover until they could locate where the gunshots were corning from. The man sitting in the passenger seat hopped over and got behind the wheel. Threw it in drive and pulled away from the curb. I took off running in pursuit of one of the shooters, a tall, skinny dude with a black ski mask covering his identity. He ran along the side of the funeral home, and into the backyard. Hopped a fence, sprinted down the alley, breathing hard and loud. The big rifle was still in his arms. All I could think about was the fact that my mother and daughter were in that funeral home. That these bitch niggas could have hit either one of them easily. That pissed me off and gave me the fuel to pursue him. I stopped and bussed, just as he stumble and dropped his AK. *Blocka. Blocka.*

The bullet sailed through the air and flipped him around. It slammed into his shoulder. He took off running, holding his right shoulder. But now, he was running slower. He looked over his shoulder at me and tried to speed up with no success. I started to run as fast as I could with my chest burning. I could barely breathe. But, I made up ground quick. Got about fifty feet away from him and bussed, aiming for his thigh, knocking a chunk out of it. It exploded and he fell to his face, just as Ajani rolled up in a Chevy Caprice Classic, blocking the alley. He hopped out with three of his Camden Boys, and started to run down the alley towards us. All of them had guns in their hands. I made it to the shooter first. Kicked him in the ass.

"Turn over, bitch, before I knock yo noodles out yo head." He whimpered. Blood spurt out of his shoulder. There was a big hole in his thigh that leaked red paint. He laid on his back and held his hands up. "Don't shoot mi, mon. Mi can help you if ya give mi de chance," he said, in a strong Jamaican accent.

# Chapter 15

Ajani slid the brass knuckles onto his fingers and fixed them so that they fit properly. He cocked back his arm, and came forward with brute force, and slammed his fist into the dread head's face, breaking his nose. I could even hear it snap. "One more time, nigga, who do you work for, and why the fuck are y'all airing at my cousin's funeral? Speak!"

I kept the flame of my blow torch on the blade of the butter knife. It was already bright red, I couldn't wait to use it. The dread head tried to catch his breath. His nose was bent awkwardly, blood oozed out of both of his nostrils, and down to his chin. He swallowed. "Mi work fah Damian, mon. He's yer wurst nightmare, and not some-body to play wiff. I follow orders or lose the life of mii family. What would you do?" he asked with his face all shiny with blood.

"What the nigga want wit me, Blood?" I asked and stepped in front of him with the red-hot butter knife. I wasn't expecting him to talk so easily. Now I was regretting lighting the knife up.

"You killed a bunch of the queens from Kingston mon. You gotta pay for yer sins. It's the Jamaican way. No way around it. He'll get you sooner or later. Damian always does."

Ajani smacked the shit out of him for no reason. "Bitch nigga, where can we find this fool at? I need addresses, home, offices, his bitch cribs, everything. And up. You al-ready got that irritating ass accent. Choking on all that blood and shit is only making the communicating process worse." I mugged him, confused. Wondering was my cousin out of his mind or what?

"Yo, where is this nigga's headquarters?" The dread head swallowed his blood and shrugged his shoulders. We had him tied to a chair in one of my trap's basements in Brooklyn.

"I tell you anything and they wipe out my entire family back in Jamaica. Mi can't risk it. Rather die as a mon, then as a coward. I've said enuff already." He swallowed again and struggled to breathe through his broken nose. Now I was happy. I placed the flame of the torch back on to the butter knife until it turned red. Then sat the canister down, and slowly applied it to the side of his cheek. It sizzled and smelled like bacon. Smoke came from it. He screamed at the top of his lungs and Ajani burst out laughing as if he were at a comedy club.

"Where the fuck can I find him!" He hopped around in his chair, crying. When I pulled the butter knife back, it had his skin stuck to it. I could see the meat on his face. It was white, before the blood started to pour out of it.

"Fucking kill me now! Kahn't take dis pain. Kill me, ya bumbaclots ! Amerikins, mii don't fuck wit ya pussy—" I lit the knife again and placed the flaming blade right on his forehead. Pressed it hard against him, and drug it downward. It sunk into his flesh like butter. I allowed for it to rest and burn him right under his right eye. His cheek had smoke drifting to the sky. Now he was really going hysterical. "Argh! Argh! Mii kahn't snitch! He'd kill mii whole family. Juss kill mii! Kill mii now!"

"Yo burn his ass again. He think we playing wit him or some thin'," Ajani said, with his upper lip curled. He took a step back and kicked the dread head in the chest so hard that he flipped over in the chair, and wound up on his side, bleeding.

When I went to reach for the canister, Ajani picked it up and started the flame. He knelt to one knee, and grabbed a handful of the shooter's dreads, starting the flame. "Say, my nigga, if you don't tell us what we need to know, I'm about to burn yo ass like Lucifer. Start talking."

The Jamaican wheezed through his nose. Struggling to breathe regularly. Blood formed all around him. "He got a spot a few blocks from the docks, right along the Delaware River. Most of his hoods operate out of the alley in Jersey. Now kill me. Kill me now, and make sure dat he knows I'm dead. Else he'll kill ma family fer mii snitching."

He turned onto his back. Ajani looked up at me. "You believe this nigga, Cuz?" I looked down on him for a long time, watching him squirm. Blood gushing out of every wound in his body. I felt no remorse for his bitch ass. Started to imagine one of those bullets that he spit hitting my mother, daughter, or Bree and Rayven. That pissed me off worse than before.

"Yeah, Blood. Smoke this nigga, kid. And toss his ass in the Harbor. Word up."

Ajani stood up. "You ain't said nothing but a word. But then, we about to go handle this Jamaican fuck nigga, right?" He asked, raising his Timb about knee high, then brought it down as hard as he could into the dread head's jaw, crushing it to the ground. The dread head seemed to bark like a dog as his face was crushed into the basement concrete. Ajani raised his Timb and stomped him over and over. Each time, he put a little more force into his stomps. By the time he finished, he'd completely smashed the dread's face inward. He lay on the floor dead, dead.

* * *

Rayven paced back and forth with a glass full of red wine. "We gotta get you some protection, Kaleb. Ain't no telling what them Jamaicans are on right now. And then, we gotta deal with Buddy. That nigga been missing in action for weeks now. I'm wondering when he's going to pop up and when he does, what he's going to be on? I think we need to get the fuck out of New York. Ain't no sense in us being here any longer. It's not safe."

I made my daughter stand up on her little feet. She placed both of them on my thighs and smiled at me, with her gray eyes. She had a dimple on each cheek. I kissed her on the forehead. "Yo, I told you about cursing in front of her. We gotta guard our tongues. Nah' mean? My baby precious." I mugged Rayven.

"Did you hear what I said, Kaleb? I think we should leave New York and go somewhere else. I mean, why are we even here to begin with? I mean, besides your mother and Derez?"

I scoffed and looked into my daughter's eyes. "I know you're a little nervous right now, but I ain't about to let nobody run me away from my homeland. New York is in my heart. Everywhere else sucks, if you ask me. Yo, we gon' find Buddy, and handle them Jamaican studs. It's only a matter of time before this war is over with, trust me on that." I picked my daughter up and made her fly over my head like Super Girl. A line of slob dropped on to my face, catching me off guard.

Rayven plopped down on the sofa next to me. "What if you wind up losing this war, Kaleb? Bullets ain't got no names on 'em. That's bad enough. But, its ten times worst when bullets really do have names on 'em, and all of them are meant for you. Every time you walk out of that door, I am sick with worry. I can't eat. I can't sleep. I can't even think straight. I'm losing weight. I can't handle this shit." She covered her mouth after she let out the swear word. Looked me over closely.

I frowned and set my daughter on my lap. Wiped her slob from my face and kissed her. "Yo, I'm naming her Destiny after my sister. You can get the middle name. You cool wit that?"

# Rise to Power 2

Rayven shook her head and slammed her fist into the palm of her hand. "Yo, why are you ignoring me, kid? You about to have me all vexed in a minute. I'm trying to be cool." She said this, jumping from the couch, staring down at me.

I rubbed a tuft of Destiny's wavy hair, then kissed her small forehead again. As long as I had my daughter in my arms, it seemed like it was impossible for me to lose my cool. Her eyes closed, and within minutes, she fell asleep in my arms. I laid her in her crib and swaddled her in her Disney Princess blanket. Kissed her forehead and made my way back into the living room, where Rayven was sitting at the table, pouring herself another glass of wine. I grabbed the bottle and took a sip out of it. "Aiight, what's yo problem now, ma? My baby sleep. Everything is good. The floor is yours." I lowered myself to the couch, looking over at her.

"I want out of New York. I want us to take our daughter to the other side of the country. Start fresh, and get into real estate over there. Maybe open a few businesses. I got a lot of money put up, and so do you. We can invest it, and see our cream add up. Ain't no sense of being in this run-down city warring with lowlifes when we have a daughter who needs us. I want out. Now, Kaleb! Things are way too dangerous. Please see it my way." I sat there with my head hung for a few minutes. Thinking things over.

I knew she made a good point. We had enough money to flee to another city and buy up properties. Flip them and accrue even more income. I could cop a few restaurants and we could make money that way as well. I honestly didn't have to pick up another pack or flip another kilo of heroin if I didn't want too. I could go all the way legit, and capitalize off of what I had been blessed with in the game so far. I wanted to be there for my daughter. Every step of the way. I knew she was going to need me, because the world was a cold place to be. It seemed like people were getting more and more cruel every single day. I would have to be around to protect her from the world.

But then, there was my mother and Derez, also Bree. They needed me as well. How could I leave them behind to go about my life? I had been there for them for as long as I could remember. I couldn't turn my back on them. It wasn't in me to. So, while some of things Rayven said made sense, it just felt like she wasn't seeing the bigger picture. "Rayven, what about my mother? What about Derez? Are they coming with us?"

She exhaled and shrugged her shoulders. "Yo, I don't know, Kaleb. Damn, we got a whole ass daughter now. When do we leave your baggage behind and focus on the baggage we have under our own roof? You can't keep trying to provide for and protect everybody. Sooner or later that stuff is going to take a toll on you. And by the way you're going, it's going to take a toll on your life because you don't know how to go soft, you always gotta go so hard. Why can't it just be our little family? Why?"

I frowned and stood up. "Because it can't. I gotta make sure my mother and my little brother stay up top! All they got is me. If I don't put the food on the table, then they don't eat. My father was a bitch-ass nigga. He ran out on us before I could even piss straight. I'll never be like him. I'd rather die than to give up on my family, or leave them to fend for themselves in New York. Only the stronger survive here, and I'm their muscle! Me! Just me!"

She shook her head. "But, you can't be their sacrifice for the rest of your life, Kaleb. Sooner or later, they are going to have to fend for themselves. You have a daughter now. I am your fiancée. You are about to be married. Damn! Nigga, you can't be a super hero to everybody. They will be alright."

"Yo, if you say that shit again, I'ma smack you in your mouth. Word up. My moms sick right now. My little brother is still reeling over Destiny's death. On top of that, he's a target. Any one of them fools see kid anywhere in the Apple slipping, they gon' knock his head off. That's what war is. So, if you're planning on fleeing like some coward, then you gon' put them chips up so my moms and brother can flee too. I ain't leaving them behind. Not now, not never. Case muthafucking closed. You understand me?" I felt my blood pressure rising.

She waved me off. "You wilding. And I like how you can sling all these curse words at me, but you want us to speak lovely around Destiny. That's a double standard. How about you have some respect for the woman that pushed her out? I been feeling like shit ever since I did. No appreciation been coming from ya ass. None, kid. That shit starting to make me feel some type of way, adding to my post-partum and all of that shit. Word up." She turned her back to me. "Don't let me find out that all you wanted from me was a child, Kaleb. Yo, I swear I'll leave you two alone to be with each other. That's on my mother."

"You always gotta be so damn dramatic. Damn, that's so un- attractive. Yo, I gotta get out of here for a second. My head is spinning too bad. You fucking me up, Rayven, as always."

"Yo, my word, I ain't start fucking you up until you started fucking Bree. After you came from between her thighs, you been acting real foul towards me, Kaleb. Yo, and it's breaking me down so bad. But I'm tired of crying. I'm tired of it. I'm to the point that I don't even care about being alone anymore. So, if you wanna run out of the door and go back to that bitch, then do it. Just go. I'm not even kidding." She walked to the door and opened it wide. I could see clear out to the street in front of the house.

A car rolled past, and a draft breezed into the house from outside. "Rayven, close the door before you let a draft in here and my baby get sick. Close the fucking door!" I snapped, rushed over and slammed it. Now Destiny was up and hollering at the top of her lungs. That irritated me even more. "Damn, it's always something with you. Don't you get tired of all of this arguing shit? That's why I don't like being around you for long periods of time. It's just exhausting. Fuck." I made my way to the room where Destiny was.

I picked her up out of the crib. She began to scream louder, until I bounced her up and down, patting her Pamper. "It's okay, mama. It's okay. Daddy right here. I ain't going nowhere. You got me, baby." I wiped tears from her little cheeks.

When I got back into the living room, Rayven, was holding a .38 Special in her hand. "All you care about is that baby, ain't it?" She put a bullet into the chamber and dropped the box on the floor. Bullets spilled out of it. She spun the chamber and snapped it in place. Cocked the hammer. I held Destiny by the back of her head, and placed her face into my chest.

"Yo, what are you doing, Rayven?"

"You don't care about me, Kaleb, it's oh so clear. All you care about is our daughter. So, why am I here?" She put the gun to her temple and pulled the trigger.

*Click!*

She took it away and spun it again. Placed it back to her temple. I looked for someplace to put Destiny. Her mother was tripping. For as long as I had known her, I'd never known her to be suicidal or attempting anything like she was doing right there in front of me and our daughter. It was blowing my mind.

I rushed Destiny back into her bedroom and placed her in her crib. As soon as I set her down, she started to scream at the top of her lungs. But, I couldn't focus on that. I had

154

to get back into the living room before Rayven killed herself. When I got back in there, I nearly had a heart attack.

T.J. Edwards

# Chapter 16

There, smack dab in the middle of the living room stood Rayven, and on the side of her was Buddy. He had a shotgun pressed up against her lips, with three of his goons from New Orleans standing behind him with red rags around their necks, and mugs on their faces. I saw the hammers on the double barrel shotgun was cocked back, and ready to be fired. One of the dudes from Buddy's crew had a handful of Rayven's hair. Her head was pulled backward at an awkward angle. The gun she'd attempted to take her life with was on the floor right in front of her. The chamber was opened on it and it appeared to have been emptied of the lone bullet she'd loaded it with. Tears ran out of her eyes. There was a big smile on Buddy's face. I felt sick.

"Well, well, well. What it do, Blood?" he asked, laughing just a bit. He raised his arm, so the shotgun was leveled against her lips. I had a .40 Glock in the small of my back, and I had visions on grabbing it and firing until it was empty. I would never let this nigga harm my daughter or take me alive. Rayven appeared to be caught up in a sticky situation. One false move and all it would take would be for him to pull the trigger. He'd blow her head right off of her neck. I'd used a double barrel shotgun on someone at close range before, it was sure to decapitate a person. I didn't want Rayven to suffer that fate. Even though minutes earlier, she was threatening to take her own life. I loved her and knew I had to protect her at all costs. I had to play things cool.

I took a step toward them and held my hands at shoulder level. "Yo, Buddy, she ain't got shit to do wit what you and I got going on, Blood. You can let her go and we can handle this shit ourselves. Nah' mean?"

He shook his head. "Nall, you see that's where you're wrong at, B. Once you crossed me. Lied to the Fam about that lil scratch and got my hand chopped off. Then, if that wasn't enough, yo trifling ass start fucking wit my baby mother behind my back. And, get the bitch pregnant. Nigga, this shit got everything to do wit this bitch right here. Since I can't find Bree, I'ma blow her shit off in her place. Then, I'ma kill that newborn bitch in that back room, before I whack yo punk ass. That's how this is going to go down. Word up," he snickered. "Unless you can convince me otherwise."

I could hear Destiny screaming at the top of her lungs. I was praying that she quieted down. I wondered if I had cursed my daughter by naming her after her aunt that had received such a tragic fate? How was I going to protect her to make sure she wouldn't have to? I couldn't drop the ball twice. I shook my head. "I done took the rap for you for plenty shit growing up. Nigga, I got three slugs in me for some drama you kicked off. Drama I ain't have nothing to do wit. But, I took them slugs like a man, because I fucked wit you the long way. They could have ended my life, but I survived, nigga. I thought—"

"Nigga, cry me a muthafucking river. What the fuck that shit got to do wit what we're faced with right now? You fucked my bitch, got my hand cut off, and stabbed me in the back. Yo, you gone have to come better than them slugs you got in ya ass right now. I'm talking you got a matter of seconds." He looked over his shoulder. "Blood, one of y'all go back there and shut that bitch up. All that screaming and shit is getting on my nerves. Word up." He smiled at me.

One of his goons made their way toward me and the bedroom. I upped my .40 Glock and cocked that bitch. "On my mother, you finna have to kill me. Ain't neither one of you bitch niggas about to lay a hand on my seed. That's my word."

I tapped the trigger and enacted the red beam on top of the gun. Placed the dot right on Buddy's forehead. His eyes trailed upward until they crossed. Tracing the beam. His boys jumped back, then upped their guns and aimed them at me. "Tell them bitch niggas to drop it, Buddy. Now! Nigga, my word, we all about to die in here," I hollered, and this seemed to make Destiny cry louder.

That made my eyes water. I had a feeling all of us were about to meet the Reaper, and although I wasn't ready to go. There was no way I could stand back and let them hurt my child. They would be forced to do that over my dead body.

"Kaleb, you pussy-ass nigga. If you don't take that beam off of my head, nigga, I'm about to blow her shit back. And you know I ain't playing, either. If I'll kill my own daughter, you know I'll kill this punk bitch." He jugged the gun into her lips, causing them to bleed. I could hear her moaning and groaning.

"Fuck nigga, you do it, and I'ma blast you. They might blast me, but I'ma knock ya memories out of ya head for sure. That's my word." I slowly came closer to him but made sure my body stayed blocking the entrance to the hallway that led to my daughter's bedroom. I was ready for an all-out gunfight. I felt like my whole life had led up to this. You live by the sword, you die by the sword. It was what it was.

Rayven wiggled her head just enough to open her lips. "Please don't do this, Buddy. We'll pay you. We'll pay you to go away. Just name your price. Then, take the money and go. Please," she whimpered, and I didn't know if I completely agreed with her.

I didn't respect this nigga, especially after what he did to my sister and his daughter. I knew I could never bow

T.J. Edwards

down and tuck my tail. I wasn't about to pay him shit. I wanted to pull the trigger and knock his head off of his neck. What happened afterward just happened. I didn't even give a fuck no more, until I thought about my defenseless baby girl in the other room. Her screaming had stopped. Now she was crying just loud enough for me to hear her. "Bitch, how much money is you talking? Huh? That shit better be way up there too. I'm talking some serious figures," Buddy spat, with saliva flying out of his mouth.

"Whatever you want. Just name your price and I'll make it happen. I promise. Nobody has to die here tonight. There has been enough killing. Please let me squash this bullshit." I curled my lip and tightened my finger over the trigger. I was seconds away from pulling it. It was shaped like a hair trigger and I was ready to pull that bitch's hair. Word.

Buddy looked over at me and lowered his eyes. "Three million, bitch. I know y'all got it. I want three million in cash, or this shit gon' only get worse." He said this through clenched teeth. Mugging me the whole time. I took two steps backward toward the hallway. My daughter had gotten awfully quiet. I worried about her. I knew that she was not past the Sudden Infant Death stage. She'd been crying and screaming so hard and loud, I worried she'd hurt herself in some way.

"Nigga, take that paper and get yo bitch ass on. It's either that or we all die here tonight. I'm letting you know right now I ain't going. I ain't giving you shit, and if you buss, I buss. I'm knocking yo shit off, and letting the cards fall where they might."

"Shut up, Kaleb. Damn. Before this crazy ass nigga kill me," Rayven cried. Her face was beet red. I could see her shaking from where I stood. I felt sorry for her. To see a nigga with a gun pressed to her face. I also pictured seeing

160

my sister's body lying in her casket. The knife wounds all over her face. The big slice in her neck that looked like an open mouth. Next to her casket was Breeyonna's. The poor baby. He'd refused to spare either of the two.

My mind started to race, and I got angry. My heart began to pound in my chest like crazy. Sweat slid down my back and stopped at the waist line of my pants. My mouth and throat were both dry, as if I'd eaten a handful of baby powder.

"Aiight, let's go, Rayven. You gon' come wit me. You get me this money, and I'll go on about my bidness and forget you two ever existed. I'll even let that new bitch live," he snickered, and eyed me with hate in his eyes. "Let's go, Blood, this bitch coming wit us." He moved from behind her and pressed the shotgun to her temple.

One of his guys opened the front door, and turned back to aim his gun at me. It took all of the restraint I had in me to not start bussing back to back. My mind flashed from my sister's funeral, then to the day of my daughter's birth. If I started shooting, I was sure to kill Buddy. That was a given. But then, he would pull his trigger and kill Rayven. One or two of his guys would hit me up, and I could die. Also one of their bullets could fly through the wall and hit my baby girl. And, even if that did not happen, after Buddy killed Rayven, I killed him, and his guys killing me. Destiny would be without parents in a cold ass world. She didn't stand a chance. I had to think logically and secure her first and for most. She was my seed. I couldn't be so stupid and callous. They slowly made their way out of the door with all eyes on me. Every time they took a step backward, I took a step forward, feeling like shit because I couldn't save my baby mother. That I was allowing the man that had killed my sister, and goddaughter to walk out of my house untouched. I felt like a pussy. Like a simp. Weak. I couldn't believe myself.

"That's right, Kaleb. Just be smooth. We gon' take this bitch, get this money and everything gon' be all right. Feel me?" Buddy asked, with his eyes lowering. Rayven whimpered. Looked me in the eyes.

"Please, just let him take me, baby. It's okay. It's okay. I'll be back in a minute." Though these words came from her mouth, I was sure I would never hear from her again. I knew Buddy would kill her as soon as he got the money, and because of that I couldn't allow for that to happen. The man in me wouldn't allow it. I turned the beam so it shined right into his left eye.

"Nall, nigga, let Rayven go. I don't trust yo punk ass. We'll drop the money off at a later time. But, let her go and tell yo niggas to drop they guns, right now."

"Kaleb, no! Please baby! Just let him take me!" she screamed.

"What! Nigga, stop playin wit me. This bitch coming wit us. When I get my money, I'll let her go. Y'all keep moving!" he ordered.

"Please, it's good, Kaleb. I'll be back. Please don't do nothin' stupid. I promise, I'll be back." I bit into my bottom lip so hard, I drew blood. I didn't know what to do. I was so confused. I watched them lead her to Buddy's Chevy Caprice, and toss her inside, before they skirted down the street, Buddy laughing at the top of his lungs.

I ran into the street, with images of Rayven and me when we were kids playing at recess going through my mind. Suddenly, the tears came. I knew I would never see her again. I broke down, right there in the middle of the street. Stayed that way for what must have been ten minutes. Until Ajani's money green Porsche pulled up. He jumped out with three of his Camden hittas and surrounded me. All of them had guns in their hands.

Ajani knelt and placed his hand on my shoulder. "Lil cuz, what's good, Blood?" He looked around, then back down to me. I made my way to my feet. Feeling sick on the stomach.

"That bitch nigga, Buddy, took Rayven. He hollering he want three million dollars. I know he about to kill my baby mother after she drop that bread, so we gotta find him first. I had my beam on that nigga head, son. I should have pulled the trigger, but he would have iced her."

Ajani blew air out of his jaws and swallowed. "Man, dawg, this shit don't get no easier," he said, running his big hand over his face. He shook his head and stopped in his tracks. I turned around to look at him. My body felt weak and drained of energy. I felt like I was missing something.

"What don't get no easier?" I asked, looking his hittas over carefully. They refused to make eye contact with me. Ajani took a deep breath and looked up at me. "Them dread heads clapped back, lil cuz. They snatched Derez and your mother and sent word that the only way you'd ever see either one again, is if you trade yourself, for both of them. The reason why I'm here right now is because I just got off of the phone with your mother. She say she sick and need her medication. I got it in the car, but I don't know which way to go. I'm sorry, kid."

I fell to my knees again, this time, I couldn't take it anymore. I broke the fuck down. It felt like all of my enemies were coming at me at once. Hitting me from every angle. I felt trapped. Lost and confused. I cried so hard I got dizzy, before I stood up to gather myself.

Ajani rubbed my back, with a mug on his face. "Yo, I got the drop on Damian. I had a few of my close ones check the move on his duck-off by the Delaware River. His headquarters is in 'The Alley', that's a drug infested spot over in New Jersey, right around Camden where my lil niggas from, and where we used to live. I know that hood like the back of my hand. My pops used to run that bitch before the Jamaicans took it over once he got indicted. Anyway, I'ma about to have the Ski Mask Cartel mount up, and take that flight out this way so we can go at these niggas head on. I got you, Blood. I'll never leave you to fend for yourself. Let's get on some bloody shit. Word up," he said, frowning.

I strolled back into the house, thinking things over. At this point, I really didn't have a choice. Muthafuckas had backed me into a corner, where the only thing that made sense was murder, and lots of it. In a matter of weeks, I had lost my sister and my goddaughter. My baby mother got snatched, and now my enemies had taken my ill mother, and baby brother. I ain't have shit to lose. I stopped in the living room and nodded to him. "It's on, nigga. These niggas think it's sweet, aiight then, let's give 'em cavities." I shook up with him and gave him a half-hug.

I walked in the direction of my daughter's room, after he turned his back and started to walk in the opposite direction. His guys stayed in the living room on security as if they had been trained properly by street savages. When I walked into the room, I felt a slight breeze. The window was wide open, causing the curtain to blow. I knew for a fact it had been shut. I made sure of that.

My heart dropped into my stomach. I slowly approached her crib afraid of what I was to find. I felt a sharp pain shoot through my chest. It hobbled me. I got dizzy and fell to my knees. My face hit the carpet. The room began to spin. I closed my eyes and whispered her name, "Destiny." I remembered how it had felt to hold her in my arms for the first time. Then everything faded to black.

*To Be Continued...*
Rise to Power 3
Coming Soon

# Submission Guideline

Submit the first three chapters of your completed manuscript to ldpsubmissions@gmail.com, subject line: Your book's title. The manuscript must be in a .doc file and sent as an attachment. Document should be in Times New Roman, double spaced and in size 12 font. Also, provide your synopsis and full contact information. If sending multiple submissions, they must each be in a separate email.

Have a story but no way to send it electronically? You can still submit to LDP/Ca$h Presents. Send in the first three chapters, written or typed, of your completed manuscript to:

**LDP: Submissions Dept**
**Po Box 870494**
**Mesquite, Tx 75187**

*DO NOT send original manuscript. Must be a duplicate.*

Provide your synopsis and a cover letter containing your full contact information.

Thanks for considering LDP and Ca$h Presents.

# T.J. Edwards

**Coming Soon from Lock Down Publications/Ca$h Presents**

BOW DOWN TO MY GANGSTA

By **Ca$h**

TORN BETWEEN TWO

By **Coffee**

BLOOD STAINS OF A SHOTTA **III**

By **Jamaica**

STEADY MOBBIN **III**

By **Marcellus Allen**

BLOOD OF A BOSS **V**

By **Askari**

LOYAL TO THE GAME **IV**

LIFE OF SIN II

By **T.J. & Jelissa**

A DOPEBOY'S PRAYER II

By **Eddie "Wolf" Lee**

IF LOVING YOU IS WRONG… **III**

LOVE ME EVEN WHEN IT HURTS **II**

By **Jelissa**

TRUE SAVAGE **VII**

By **Chris Green**

BLAST FOR ME **III**

A BRONX TALE III

DUFFLE BAG CARTEL II

By **Ghost**

ADDICTIED TO THE DRAMA **III**

By **Jamila Mathis**

LIPSTICK KILLAH **III**

166

# Rise to Power 2

Mimi

WHAT BAD BITCHES DO **III**

A HUSTLER'S DECEIT 3

KILL ZONE **II**

By **Aryanna**

THE COST OF LOYALTY **II**

By **Kweli**

SHE FELL IN LOVE WITH A REAL ONE **II**

By **Tamara Butler**

RENEGADE BOYS **III**

By **Meesha**

CORRUPTED BY A GANGSTA **IV**

By **Destiny Skai**

A GANGSTER'S CODE **III**

By **J-Blunt**

KING OF NEW YORK IV

RISE TO POWER III

By **T.J. Edwards**

GORILLAS IN THE BAY II

**De'Kari**

THE STREETS ARE CALLING II

**Duquie Wilson**

KINGPIN KILLAZ III

**Hood Rich**

STEADY MOBBIN' **III**

**Marcellus Allen**

SINS OF A HUSTLA II

**ASAD**

TRIGGADALE II

# T.J. Edwards
### Elijah R. Freeman
MARRIED TO A BOSS II

### By Destiny Skai & Chris Green
KINGS OF THE GAME II

### Playa Ray


### Available Now
RESTRAINING ORDER **I & II**

### By **CA$H & Coffee**
LOVE KNOWS NO BOUNDARIES **I II & III**

### By **Coffee**
RAISED AS A GOON I, II,  III & IV

BRED BY THE SLUMS I, II, III

BLAST FOR ME I & II

ROTTEN TO THE CORE I III

A BRONX TALE I, II

### By **Ghost**
LAY IT DOWN **I & II**

LAST OF A DYING BREED

BLOOD STAINS OF A SHOTTA I & II

### By **Jamaica**
LOYAL TO THE GAME

LOYAL TO THE GAME II

LOYAL TO THE GAME III

LIFE OF SIN

### By **TJ & Jelissa**
BLOODY COMMAS I & II

SKI MASK CARTEL I  II & III

168

# Rise to Power 2

T.J. Edwards
By **Destiny Skai**

WHEN A GOOD GIRL GOES BAD

By **Adrienne**

A GANGSTER'S REVENGE **I II III & IV**

THE BOSS MAN'S DAUGHTERS

THE BOSS MAN'S DAUGHTERS II

THE BOSSMAN'S DAUGHTERS III

THE BOSSMAN'S DAUGHTERS IV

THE BOSS MAN'S DAUGHTERS **V**

A SAVAGE LOVE **I & II**

BAE BELONGS TO ME

A HUSTLER'S DECEIT I, II, III

WHAT BAD BITCHES DO I, II

By **Aryanna**

A KINGPIN'S AMBITON

A KINGPIN'S AMBITION **II**

I MURDER FOR THE DOUGH

By **Ambitious**

TRUE SAVAGE

TRUE SAVAGE II

TRUE SAVAGE **III**

TRUE SAVAGE **IV**

TRUE SAVAGE **V**

TRUE SAVAGE **VI**

By **Chris Green**

A DOPEBOY'S PRAYER

By **Eddie "Wolf" Lee**

THE KING CARTEL **I, II & III**

By **Frank Gresham**

170

# Rise to Power 2

THESE NIGGAS AIN'T LOYAL **I, II & III**

By **Nikki Tee**

GANGSTA SHYT **I II &III**

By **CATO**

THE ULTIMATE BETRAYAL

By **Phoenix**

BOSS'N UP **I , II & III**

By **Royal Nicole**

I LOVE YOU TO DEATH

**By Destiny J**

I RIDE FOR MY HITTA

I STILL RIDE FOR MY HITTA

By **Misty Holt**

LOVE & CHASIN' PAPER

By **Qay Crockett**

TO DIE IN VAIN

**SINS OF A HUSTLA**

By **ASAD**

BROOKLYN HUSTLAZ

By **Boogsy Morina**

BROOKLYN ON LOCK I & II

By **Sonovia**

GANGSTA CITY

By **Teddy Duke**

A DRUG KING AND HIS DIAMOND I & II III

A DOPEMAN'S RICHES

HER MAN, MINE'S TOO I, II

CASH MONEY HO'S

**By Nicole Goosby**

# T.J. Edwards

TRAPHOUSE KING **I II & III**

KINGPIN KILLAZ

By **Hood Rich**

LIPSTICK KILLAH **I, II**

CRIME OF PASSION I & II

By **Mimi**

STEADY MOBBN' **I, II**

By **Marcellus Allen**

WHO SHOT YA **I, II**

**Renta**

GORILLAZ IN THE BAY

**DE'KARI**

TRIGGADALE

**Elijah R. Freeman**

GOD BLESS THE TRAPPERS I, II, III

THESE SCANDALOUS STREETS I, II, III

FEAR MY GANGSTA I, II, III

THESE STREETS DON'T LOVE NOBODY I, II

BURY ME A G I, II, III, IV, V

**Tranay Adams**

THE STREETS ARE CALLING

**Duquie Wilson**

MARRIED TO A BOSS…

By **Destiny Skai & Chris Green**

KINGS OF THE GAME II

**Playa Ray**

**BOOKS BY LDP'S CEO, CA$H**

TRUST IN NO MAN

TRUST IN NO MAN 2

TRUST IN NO MAN 3

BONDED BY BLOOD

SHORTY GOT A THUG

THUGS CRY

THUGS CRY 2

THUGS CRY 3

TRUST NO BITCH

TRUST NO BITCH 2

TRUST NO BITCH 3

TIL MY CASKET DROPS

RESTRAINING ORDER

RESTRAINING ORDER 2

IN LOVE WITH A CONVICT

**Coming Soon**

BONDED BY BLOOD 2

BOW DOWN TO MY GANGSTA

T.J. Edwards

www.ingramcontent.com/pod-product-compliance
Lightning Source LLC
Chambersburg PA
CBHW070033260626
47159CB00005B/2026